TOM GAINES

Quantum Dagger

First published by Harborstone Press 2024

This novel is entirely a work of fiction. The names, characters and incidents portrayed in it are the work of the author's imagination. Any resemblance to actual persons, living or dead, events or localities is entirely coincidental.

First edition

ISBN: 979-8-9916074-0-7

Chapter 1

Matt clipped the second leg strap of his parachute harness and looked up to see the Air Force loadmaster wading through the C-17's cargo-filled cabin back to where he and Dean were rigging themselves up to jump.

"Flight deck says we have ten minutes until we're at the release point," the loadmaster said. "I'm going to wait until about two minutes out before opening the ramp, though. It's cold out there at thirty thousand feet. No sense in freezing any more than we have to."

Dean gave him the thumbs-up before feeding the last bit of webbing through the buckle on his chest strap. Over the next few minutes, the two men finished adjusting all their equipment and took turns inspecting each other's rigging. Matt had gone through this ritual dozens of times before and had it down by the numbers, but this was different. This wasn't for training. He didn't have time to think about his nerves right now, so he buried the thought where it wouldn't interfere with the task at hand. Dean was one of the most experienced operatives in the unit, and the two had rehearsed every part of the mission until he was confident that they were ready. Besides, Matt thought, snapping his oxygen mask into place and turning the valve on the bottle to open, this was the easy part. Through the dim green light, he saw the loadmaster give them the warning signal and flip the switch to lower the ramp.

Walking to the edge of the opening, Dean leaned over to peek between the ramp and the fuselage and check the conditions outside the aircraft. He pulled himself off the floor and turned, giving a thumbs-up to the loadmaster. "It's about as good as we're going to get, brother," he said to Matt. "What do you say we kick this thing off?"

Matt gave him a fist bump, and stared at the indicator light, willing it to turn green. In the cockpit, the navigation system chimed, indicating that they had reached their mark. Checking his instruments one last time, the pilot flipped a switch, and the drop light came alive. *Well, we didn't come all this way for nothing*, Matt thought, stepping out into the unknown.

Skydiving is an adrenaline sport, but after a minute of freefall Matt was almost bored. As fast as the needle on his altimeter was moving, it seemed to be taking forever to get down to four thousand feet. Mercifully, the dial finally reached the magic number, and Matt reached back, grabbed his pilot chute, and threw it out to the side. The reassuring jerk against his harness told him it was a good deployment. Looking up to inspect the canopy and find the control toggles, Matt gained control of his parachute and began steering it toward the landing zone. Once on the right heading, he looked up to find Dean gliding silently in his usual . . . *wait, where's Dean? He should be right there. He's always right there.*

Scanning the moonless night sky, Matt strained to catch a glimpse of his partner, but came up empty. As he piloted his parachute gently toward the sea, he began running through the list of possible reasons why he couldn't find Dean. Most were bad. Matt's feet caught the water, sending him crashing face-first into a rising wave. Night landings were always more of a surprise, and trying to figure out where Dean was had broken his concentration, making this one of his worst. Inflating his flotation device, Matt slid out of his harness, strapped on his fins, and pulled the line-of-sight locator from his shoulder pocket.

Oh, thank God, Dean's beacon is on. He exhaled deeply, releasing some of the anxiety that had been mounting over the past several minutes. Swimming toward the indicator, Matt steeled himself for what he would find.

"Holy hell, that hurt!"

"Dean? Are you OK?"

"Yeah, brother. Well, no, not really, but I'm alive. My main cigarette rolled, and I burned in. I don't remember the impact, but fortunately I came to before everything got waterlogged and sank. Something is wrong with my legs, though. I can feel them and move them, but they hurt like hell when I do."

Matt closed the distance homing in on Dean's voice. In the darkness, he didn't spot Dean's body bobbing lightly in the swell until he was almost on top of him. Taking out his knife, Matt began cutting away the risers to free his injured partner from the parachute. As the canopy drifted away, Matt could see that Dean's legs twisted and dangling beneath him. "Man, I didn't know what happened to you. I looked up where you always were and saw nothing but stars."

"Murphy's law rears its ugly head once more, huh?" Dean said, grimacing.

"I'll say. Where the hell is the boat?"

"Should be here. We've got our short-range beacons on. He'll find us."

No sooner had the words rolled out of Dean's mouth than

the faint rumble of a marine diesel rose out of the darkness. Matt pulled out his flashlight, flipped on the infrared filter, and pulsed the far-recognition symbol in the direction of the sound. The pair waited as the engine noise grew louder until finally they could make out the weathered hull of a small fishing trawler. Giving the signal once more, Matt positioned himself between the boat and his injured partner, and drew the Glock from its holster. The boat slowed, cutting its engine as it pulled alongside the two men.

"Little dark for a swim, isn't it?" came a voice from the aft deck.

"Best way to catch the fish sleeping," Matt returned, completing the near-recognition pattern.

"Welcome to the Philippines."

"Manny, shut up and help me in the boat!" Dean shouted.

"Well, what's got you all bothered tonight?" asked Manny.

"Burned in. I think he's pretty jacked up. Help me get him up out of the water so we can see what we're working with," Matt said quickly as he swam the pair to the back of the boat.

Manny stepped down onto the stern platform. Matt unclipped his and Dean's assault bags and handed them up, timing each with the sea swell. After pushing the bags farther up the deck and out of the way, Manny turned back and, grabbing Dean by the shoulder straps of his harness, hauled the injured man out of the water.

Dean gasped in pain. "Jesus, Manny, think you could have thrown me around any harder? I don't think I'm quite broken in two yet."

"You know what Doc always says: pain is the patient's problem. I could put you back if you'd prefer." Manny knelt over the man lying on the deck and began assessing his injuries as Matt climbed up the ladder and removed the rest of his kit. "Are you going to stand there dripping on me, Matt, or do you want to help me figure out what kind of mess Dean's gotten himself into?"

"Sorry."

"It's OK. You start with the feet. I'll start with the head."

Manny and Matt ran through their triage sequence, checking for bleeding or other signs of physical trauma. When he got to Dean's hips, Matt gently pressed both sides. Despite his best efforts to remain stoic, Dean howled in pain.

"Feels crunchy. I'm pretty sure your hip's shattered," Matt said to Dean, turning to look at Manny. "We need to get him out of here. I'll finish up stabilizing him if you want to start taking us in. I need to call the boss. This whole thing just went south."

-

Matt terminated the connection, powered off the radio, and slid it into the small pouch on the outside of his bag, pausing to watch the rising sun dip in and out of view behind the rolling waves. He turned and walked into the cabin. Passing through the door, he finally got a good look at his partner in the light. Dean was pale and in obvious pain, but still managed a reassuring smile.

"Well, what'd the boss have to say?" Dean asked.

"He left it up to us. We're the team on the ground and have the best handle on the situation."

Dean attempted to sit up, quickly recognized his error, and lay back down. "Let's talk it through. What do we know?"

"I mean, the situation is still the same. Over the past eighteen months, we've had our asses handed to us four times by the Chinese."

"That we know about."

"That we know about," Matt corrected. "First, in less than a month they took out 90 percent of our recruited assets in mainland China, completely dismantling our human intelligence network in the country. Next, there was that trade negotiation with the Nigerians that broke down for seemingly no good reason, followed swiftly by the announcement that they had signed a deal with Beijing instead. Five months after that, the PLA rolls out their latest long-range drone, which is identical to the one Lockheed has been developing for the past four years that hadn't even been announced yet. And then two months ago Iranian-backed Shia militant groups claimed to have hacked into the Iraqi prime minister's office and released some unsavory information a week before their elections, all but guaranteeing the pro-US government would be out. The Chinese pretty much gloated about that one as retaliation for President Sanderson's tariff announcement."

"And?"

"And," Matt continued, "nobody in the DOD or the intelligence community has any idea what's going on. It's like the Chinese just suddenly hold all the keys and turn them at a time and place of their choosing. Of course, every analyst has a theory grasping at straws for any correlations, but nothing really makes any sense."

"Never underestimate the power of nerds to piece together the craziest connections to prove some wild theory they have. Those guys are even better than baseball statisticians. 'The fifth-year starter for the Braves is 2-10 against left-handed batters in the month of August when playing on fields that face to the east,' " Dean said in his best Bob Uecker impersonation. "And. . ."

"And now one of these analysts linked a human intelligence report about some weird equipment showing up in his telecommunications server room a few days ago in Manila to reports that our guys are getting trounced at the Southeast Asian Trade Summit going on across town. Not exactly a smoking gun."

"But," Dean said, "it's at least a theory we can act on—if we can get in there before the summit ends in two days. To meet that window, we don't have time to bring in anyone else."

"This was our shot," Matt agreed.

"This is our shot," Dean corrected. "Just because I'm useless to the project doesn't mean we have to cancel. You know the plan, and you're better at the technical side of things than me anyways."

"But we've got to get you evacuated."

"Manny can do it. Exit corridor bravo is pretty much this infil route in reverse anyways."

"Sure, I can," Manny chimed in. Matt had almost forgotten the man was sitting there, piloting the boat as it slid past a rocky outcropping. "Look, I've been here for eight months working my project out of the embassy, and Colonel Banks didn't even blink when he pulled me off of it to support you two. This thing has them spooked. You'll be fine. Dean is fine. I've got all the medical supplies I need on board anyways, so once I drop you off it'll be easy to babysit him for two days while we wait for the extraction window."

"You're right, but it still makes me nervous," Matt admitted.

"This is a clandestine special operation," Dean replied. "If you're not feeling any nerves, then there's something wrong. Now grab my bag and take anything you might find useful.

Manny, be a pal and hook me up with some of those good painkillers. I want to take a nap." Dean pulled his faded Red Sox baseball cap over his face and closed his eyes.

Matt got up from the table and walked across the cabin, grabbing the back of Manny's seat to steady himself. "You sure he's going to be OK?"

Manny looked over at Dean. "Yeah, man, I was a medic on the teams before crossing over to the unit. He's probably looking at surgery and a bunch of physical therapy, but he'll be good until we can get him into a hospital. I'll keep him company. I owe him one from this thing back in Afghanistan anyways. Now I get to repay the favor. We've got about thirty minutes until we make it back to the dock. We should hit the gap between the fishing boats all heading out and the rest of the harbor opening up, but the sooner we can get you on the road, the better. It's a solid twelve hours from here down to your hotel."

Matt emptied the team's bags onto the table. Moving Dean's change of clothes off to the side, he spread the remaining items out and began trying to figure out what he would need from his partner's kit. Since they had an asset with building access, it was likely that the only thing he would really need was the technical forensic gear, but you could never be sure. Matt slowly packed everything for the next two days back into his bag, and then consolidated the rest into Dean's.

As Manny tied off the stern line, Matt hopped off the boat and down the dock. Stepping up onto the gravel, he saw the gray Suzuki Sidekick parked right where it was supposed to be. Something about seeing it immediately calmed Matt's nerves. *The plan is back on track*, he thought, pulling out of the parking space. *Now I just have to execute.*

—

After five hours of playing tourist, Matt sat in the Suzuki outside a small grocery store waiting for the linkup time, confident that he didn't have anyone following him. Not that that meant he wasn't being surveilled. Manila, like most major cities around the world, had cameras everywhere. Security cameras, traffic cameras, emergency-response cameras. All connected to the internet. If someone had access to their collective vantage points, it didn't really matter how solid Matt's countersurveillance tradecraft was. They would simply sit back from an air-conditioned room and watch him run around the city. He knew, though, that since he and Dean had circumvented the initial facial-recognition grab by Philippine customs at the airport, it was unlikely that he was on anyone's radar.

More than anything, however, the route had helped him shake off some of the anxiety that had steadily built up since finding Dean. Something about the ritual of the tradecraft calmed him down. Every turn, every stop helped him feel more in control and on plan. There was also the familiarity of it, which brought back memories of the successful runs he'd had throughout the operator training course. Just like with the jump, this might have been his first real operation, but it wasn't the first time he had gone through this process.

Slowly edging into the evening traffic, Matt worked his way down the crowded city street toward the gas station at the end of the block. As he pulled in, he could see what should be his guy. Short-sleeved white button-down shirt and khaki pants, the uniform of mid-level IT technicians the world over, and a folded newspaper in his right hand. Matt stopped in front of him and leaned slightly out of the window.

"Excuse me, am I anywhere close to Fort Santiago?" Matt asked.

"Oh no, but I can get you there in thirty minutes," the man replied, closing the recognition exchange. "Hop in."

Matt watched as the man walked around to the passenger side and sat down. Although they were meeting for the first time, Matt could see that his contact had experience working with people like him. Checking his surroundings one more time, Matt exited the gas station and started his route.

"I'm Matt. Nice to meet you."

"Pleased to meet you, Matt. I'm Jacob."

"Did you have any issues getting here today? Notice anything peculiar?"

"No, I had no issues. No one followed me. I thought there were supposed to be two of you," Jacob replied.

Recognizing the familiar pattern of how these meetings always started, Matt began to relax. "My partner ended up getting pulled somewhere else. It's just you and me tonight, Jacob. Remember our story for why we're going into the building tonight?"

"Yes," Jacob answered, "I have an off-hours patch to perform that I had been putting off. You are a consulting rep for the monitoring software we use here to help make sure our update goes smoothly."

"Perfect. If something goes south and we get separated, go back to your normal routine and contact us through your usual means. Got it?"

"Got it."

"Tell me about what you found," Matt continued.

"I don't know what I've found," Jacob admitted. "Two weeks

ago, my boss's boss's boss walked into my office and introduced me to some Huawei representative. He had approved the trial of a new on-prem analytics server of some sort, and ordered me to get the Huawei people anything they needed. They asked for an entire rack near the main egress point for the building. I had to deinstall a couple backup routers and test servers to make room. They wheeled in a transport case, and installed one thing that didn't take up more than 15 percent of the rack. The technicians told me that they tend to run a little hot, but not to touch it even if it did. I was about to argue about the wasted space, but the look this guy gave me told me he wasn't going to entertain any push back."

"OK, but that's not too out of the ordinary for a field-testing engineer."

"You're right. Nothing was out of the ordinary. I almost forgot about it. Until it turned on. First, the power usage monitor started screaming, because the server room was suddenly consuming 400 percent more power than normal. A few minutes later, the environmental monitor joined in as well. I went down to check on the system, and it was ridiculously hot. I called my manager and warned him that I might have to take the test server offline. Twenty seconds later, the COO himself called. He told me that if I touch anything on that system, I'm fired, and to just do whatever I have to do to keep everything running. Any additional expenses to do so were authorized by him personally."

"That's weird," Matt said.

"So, I brought in some additional cooling units, and signaled for an emergency meeting with you all."

"Well, we'll see what we can find."

The conversation trailed off and the two rode in silence until

Matt signaled his turn into the alley beside the World Telecom tower. "Are you ready?" he asked as he backed the small jeep in next to a mound of broken-down cardboard boxes.

"No sweat," Jacob answered, reassuring himself.

Matt got out of the car and walked alongside Jacob as they made their way toward the front entrance. The normal eight-to-six crowd had cleared out from the business district in favor of the local bars, but there were still enough stragglers along the sidewalks that the two didn't look out of place. Jacob badged open the front door and motioned Matt inside. At the small reception desk, the uninterested security guard waved broadly in the direction of a clipboard without taking his eyes off his phone. Jacob took a pen out of his pocket and scribbled an entry for his visitor before turning and heading for the elevators farther down the lobby.

After the elevator doors had closed, Jacob turned to Matt. "Everybody treats their IT techs like we're invisible, or just part of the office furniture. It's the weirdest thing. I can't tell you the things I've learned from people having conversations while I am clearly sitting in their office fixing their computers."

Matt smiled. "Pretty convenient for us tonight, though."

The elevator chimed open. The two men were greeted by a rush of warm air and a cacophony of fans and compressors.

"It's been steadily getting worse since that system came online," Jacob said, leading Matt down the last row. At the end, Matt could see the nearly empty server rack Jacob had mentioned, with a single box hung in the middle. As they approached, it became more and more apparent that this thing was the source of all the heat in the room.

"Jesus," Matt said as he started looking around the area. "I've never seen a server run this hot before. It's causing some of the paint to peel off of the side rails here."

Taking out his phone, Matt tapped in the pass code to open the camera app from the device's secure partition and began documenting. It looked like an ordinary computer server—a black metallic case connected only by a power cable and a single fiber-optic line. Besides the heat, Matt would never have noticed anything was out of the ordinary. Moving to the back, Matt found the case secured with four tamper-resistant screws. He pulled a screwdriver from his bag and inserted a specially designed bit. Matt carefully removed the screws, set them on the magnet attached to the side of the screwdriver's shaft, and slid back the top of the device using a jacket from his bag to insulate his hand.

Setting the cover on the floor, Matt stood back up and looked inside the case. "What the hell? It's a mess." Matt could see what looked like multiple processors, solid-state memory drives, and RAM chips, but all of them had warped out of shape as the fiberglass circuit boards holding them in place melted down. In the center was a black device six inches in diameter. Even if it hadn't been destroyed by the heat, whatever this was didn't look like any electronic component Matt had seen. After taking photos of the inside of the device, he put the phone back in his pocket and pulled out a small knife. Using the blade, he carefully probed the device, trying to get a better look at how it was constructed, but to no avail. The entire thing had melted past the point where anything could be recognized. He pried off a chunk of the center cube and put it into a small container.

"I have so many questions, but I don't think we're going to get any more answers here," Matt said. "None of the gear I've brought does any good with this heap of goo. I'm going to close up and we can get out of here." He replaced the top of the case and inserted the four security screws.

The two men walked back to the elevator, riding it up to the lobby. Matt had taken two steps out of the elevator before realizing that the lobby was no longer empty. Standing at the security desk were three Chinese men dressed in suits. One of them was holding up some form of identification and shouting something across the semicircular desk. To help make his point to the guard, the man gestured down the lobby toward the elevators, and as he did so brought the gaze of all three of the men directly in line with Matt and Jacob.

Recognition flashed across all five men's faces simultaneously, and the three Chinese men moved toward Matt and Jacob, shouting something in Mandarin.

"Back stairwell!" Matt grabbed Jacob, pulling him into action as the pair turned and ran. Matt could hear more shouting as the three men broke into pursuit. Matt shoved open the door to the stairwell, causing it to rebound off the concrete wall behind and almost knock Jacob flat. The two rushed down the stairs and through the exit door on the lower level, bursting onto the street behind the building. An alarm wailed from inside the building. Matt sprinted toward the alley where they'd parked the car with Jacob right on his heels. As they rounded the corner, he saw two of their pursuers rush out of the building, pause to find their bearings, and break into a run again once they identified which way their quarry had gone.

Jumping into the driver's seat, Matt turned the ignition and had the car in gear before Jacob had made it all the way inside. In the rear view, he watched as the two men rounded the corner, stopped running, and talking into what he assumed was a radio. His assumption was validated moments later when he pulled onto the street to find a large black SUV bearing down on them. Swerving to avoid a collision, Matt changed course, cutting across the street to continue down an alley. The driver of the black SUV slammed its brakes and turned to follow. Speeding down the alley, Matt grasped for a plan. He knew that there was no way his four-cylinder Suzuki would ever be able to outrun the more powerful SUV, so he would have to find some other way to lose them in the city. Although it was nearly 11 p.m., the amount of traffic still on the streets wasn't going to be of any help.

Matt turned sharply out of the alley and onto a surface street and weaved in and out of traffic. Three more erratic turns, and he still hadn't been able to shake his tail. It was only a matter of time before the help they were sure to have called in would arrive. A moment before panic set in, Matt saw his opening. On the other side of the intersection up ahead was an open plaza segmented off from the traffic by a row of brushed-metal bollards. Accelerating as hard as he could, Matt drove the little SUV through the gap between two of the bollards, sacrificing some paint as the car scraped by. As he continued down the pedestrian walkway, Matt saw that the larger SUV was unable to clear the barriers and had come to a halt. He turned a corner, reentering a roadway, and sped off, making two more turns in quick succession to ensure his pursuers had been unable to follow. Out of immediate danger, Matt slowed to match the pace of the other cars.

"Holy shit," Jacob exhaled. "Where did those guys come from?"

"Probably Chinese MSS—the Ministry of State Security. Generally bad news whenever they turn up. It didn't look like they were there on a routine visit, either. They must have had some sort of intrusion-detection setup I tripped poking around the system. Whatever they're up to, they caught a good look at both of us. You're not going to be safe in Manila. At least for the time being. Looks like you've got yourself a ticket to the States, if you want it."

"I'm not sure I have a choice. I don't think I want to run into them again," Jacob said.

"Good decision. I've got a place for us to hide out while I coordinate for a ride out of here. There's a bunch of people back in DC that are going to want to talk to both of us. Maybe they'll have some answers."

Chapter 2

"Where do you want this box of books?" Ish asked, trying not to let the strain of carrying it show.

"Put it next to the bookcase. Oh, wait, we don't have a bookcase, because you wouldn't let me buy the one we saw on Facebook," Drew said. Moving past him into the kitchen, she set down a container filled with dishes the two had acquired from cafeterias on campus.

Dropping the books in the corner of their new living room, Ish eyed her. "First of all, that thing was on its last legs. I'm pretty sure its structural integrity was entirely reliant on the stickers plastered all over it. Second, there was a fifty-fifty chance that that dude was going to murder us in his basement. I didn't suffer through Dr. Doom's neural-network-design class only to be shoved into a vat of acid three weeks after graduation. Hard pass."

"I'd take the acid vat over another semester having to sit in the same classroom as He-Who-Shall-Not-Be-Named, though."

"Still not over it, huh?"

"You mean after he broke up with me and almost got me kicked out of school within the span of two weeks right before Christmas? Nope, still not over it," Drew said. "I'm so freaking glad to be done with that place."

"It wasn't that bad. You met me, after all. There you were, wandering through McBryde Hall at the beginning of freshman year like a lost puppy. I don't think you would have ever found your calc classroom if I hadn't swooped in like a capeless superhero and saved you."

"More like hapless weirdo, if I remember correctly. Sometimes I don't know how either of us survived that first semester."

"Yeah, but once we got rolling, we were unstoppable. And now look at us. DARPA right out of the gate? Are you serious? If we play our cards right, we can take our pick of any graduate program in the country," Ish said.

"Maybe you can, Mr. Advanced Operational Decision-Making Project. I'm not sure training underwater drones to find and eat seaweed for fuel is going to have the same sort of paradigm-shifting impact on society."

"What can I say? They clearly recognize my skills. Still, robofish beats writing backend architecture at TurboTax." Ish ducked to avoid the pillow Drew launched at his face.

"Let me wallow in self-pity for a moment, please. And grab the other end of this table."

"No way," Ish said as the two navigated the table into the elevator. "I refuse to let you rain on your own parade. I worked way too hard molding you into the engineer you are today to do anything other than bask in my monumental accomplishment."

"If I thought for one second you believed half of the crap that comes out of your mouth, I would throw something way harder than a pillow at your head," Drew said.

"Do that. I'll lie on the couch and watch you unload the rest of the trailer."

"You're not getting off that easily. It was your idea to move into our new place the day before we start work. I don't care what you do in your half of the apartment, but as soon as the last thing is unloaded this engineer is going to bed."

-

Frank Gonzales looked out the window of his small room and let out a long exhale before tossing his phone onto the desk in front of him. Kathy was right, of course, he was beginning to sound like a broken record. How many more exercises, training events, and temporary-duty assignments would it take for him to finally realize that he wasn't finding the sense of purpose he had spent the past seven years—eleven if you counted West Point—searching for?

His entire life he'd heard stories about how his father had helped people from Grenada, East Africa, and Afghanistan build better lives and how his grandfather had spent years in Vietnam and Cambodia doing the same thing. And now here he was: a third-generation Special Forces team leader. But his fight wasn't with communists or religious zealots. Instead, he was sent on Joint Combined Exchange Training missions working alongside foreign militaries to develop their skills. Not that there was no merit to these engagements, but Frank wanted to join his family tradition as a warrior. And without a war to fight, he had a hard time making sense of all the time spent away from Kathy and their three-year-old daughter, Kyra. So this would be his last deployment. He and Kathy had agreed that he would resign his commission when he returned to Fort Lewis next month. Still unsure about the decision they'd just reached, Frank grabbed his beret and headed out the door.

"Morning, sunshine," Master Sergeant John Rizzo greeted him as he stepped into the Toyota pickup.

"Is that for me?" Frank asked, pointing at one of the coffee cups in the middle of the cab.

"Can't have my captain falling asleep on the job now, can I? How would that look?"

"John Rizzo, fending off international incidents one mediocre cup of coffee at a time."

"You can be my plus-one to Sweden when the Nobel committee realizes all the good I've done. How's Kathy?"

"She's good. Kyra is driving her nuts with some new sing-along video."

"Oh dear Lord, I do not miss that stage," Rizzo laughed.

"If there's a bright side to sweating my ass off halfway around the world, it's that I've been spared having the words to one more terrible kids' song seared in my psyche." Frank downed some of the coffee and nodded out the windshield toward the training range coming into view. "How are we doing today?"

"No issues. The platoon is itching to ditch the dry-fire runs we've been running through for live ammunition. Mac's got their Sergeant Tran dialed in, so everything should be good to go. No surprise, though, these Vietnamese Rangers are always squared away."

The truck rolled to a stop in line with the rest of the vehicles at the edge of the training area, and the two men stepped out. Frank pulled his pistol belt from the back seat and clipped it around his waist. He then drew his pistol, pressing the slide back slightly to ensure there was still a round in the chamber. Smoothing his beret into place on top of his head, Frank walked up to the formation of Vietnamese soldiers preparing for the day.

"Good morning, Captain," a heavily accented voice called out.

"Lieutenant Nguyen," Frank replied automatically, "great to see you. How are the boys today?"

Although Frank had six inches and eighty pounds on his counterpart, there was a quiet confidence in the man that told him the Vietnamese platoon leader would be a formidable opponent. He had grown up listening to his grandfather's stories of serving in the Vietnam War. One constant theme of the stories was how much the old man admired the strength and determination of the people he had fought alongside, and Frank could see what his father saw in the man standing in front of him now. With men like Lieutenant Nguyen running around it was no wonder how the Vietnamese had given the French and Americans such a hard fight sixty years ago, and no wonder why they were refusing to back down from Chinese intimidation in recent trade negotiations. Frank never could stand a bully, and seeing the Vietnamese prime minister kick the Chinese delegation out of the country for their heavy-handed tactics brought a huge smile to Frank's face.

"They are ready to go, Captain. Sergeant Mackinzie and Sergeant Tran are prepared to instruct the battle drills."

"Well, let's get to it then."

Sergeant Tran barked at the assembled soldiers, and got an immediate response as the forty men gathered around a whiteboard propped up on the side of a jeep. Once they had settled, they began talking through the squad attack drills. Standing with his counterpart behind the platoon, Frank watched both the instructors and the platoon quietly evaluating everything. Staff Sergeant Brian Mackinzie's Vietnamese was a little shocking to hear from the mouth of a Georgian farm boy. Frank kept up a basic proficiency in his assigned language of Tagalog along with the French he'd studied in school, but Mac's Vietnamese was nearly flawless as he traded off instructional points with Tran. Although technically the team's medic, Mac was just as tactically proficient as anyone else on the twelve-man team, so his command of the local language made him the obvious choice to lead the instruction. Combined with the lieutenant's English, gleaned from university studies and a ravenous consumption of American pop culture, Frank's team had had no problems overcoming the communication challenges that often plagued these exchanges.

After talking over the drills on the whiteboard, the platoon broke up into their assigned squads. Each of the squad leaders gathered his soldiers around to further translate what they had learned into the specifics for how he wanted them to operate. Since it was a squad-level event, Frank was interested to see how each man would work through the scenario. Over the next hour, he watched disciplined army processes unfolded around him as squad leaders and team leaders inspected equipment, corrected deficiencies, and rehearsed. Preparations winding down, Rizzo grabbed Gary and Tim, the team's two weapons sergeants, and drove off down a dirt path to make sure the pop-up targets spread throughout the jungle live-fire lane were set up and functioning properly.

Walking through the jungle is a fairly straightforward proposition. Slowly pick your way through the dense undergrowth while trying not to trip over any of the thousands of roots or branches. Doing this in coordination with ten other men while also hunting down a thinking, breathing enemy, though, is a completely different experience. Frank shadowed the squad as they moved toward their objective, and he could tell they were completely at ease navigating the terrain.

At the front of the formation, the alpha team leader signaled the squad to halt. In unison, each member silently knelt down and scanned the jungle around them. Frank watched as the squad leader moved up to join the team leader at the front. When he was ten feet away, Frank keyed his radio, signaling Rizzo to activate the first set of targets simulating enemy contact. The jungle erupted with gunfire as the lead team shot their targets.

The squad leader dove down next to the team leader, and the two quickly devised their plan between bursts of fire designed to keep the enemy in place. The squad leader maneuvered the second half of his force around to the side of the suspected enemy position. After one final radio call to alpha team, the squad leader led the final assault, bounding across the enemy position and engaging targets as they appeared. With the threat successfully neutralized, Frank turned to Lieutenant Nguyen.

"All right, have them cease fire. Let's clear weapons and move back to the staging area to talk through how it went."

Lieutenant Nguyen nodded and relayed the message to the squad leader.

"Not bad," Frank said as the two officers walked along the trail. "They could use a little more violence of action to help them gain fire superiority, but overall, I'd call that a success. Let's see how the other three squads shake out."

-

General Cantrell sat silently at the head of the conference-room table. This was the first time Matt had met the SOCOM commander, but he could tell that the general responsible for every special operation carried out by the Department of Defense was not happy.

"So, to recap," Cantrell said, looking down the table to Colonel Banks, "We biffed the jump, found a melted puddle of failed technology, got chased off by someone, and compromised one of our HUMINT assets. And the payoff for our troubles is what?"

Colonel Banks took a deep breath. "Sir, you know as well as I do that what we do is risky. Any of the individual pieces that went into this operation far exceed the risk threshold of pretty much anyone else on the planet. My boys put together a plan on two days' notice, flying halfway around the planet to confirm or deny a theory about what the Chinese have been up to. How many dry holes did you and I hit on our raids back in Iraq? The only thing that is certain in this game is that our adversaries are up to something."

Invoking their previous assignments together had the intended effect, and Cantrell's face softened. "You're right, JB, but where does that leave us? I'm accompanying the secretary of defense into a meeting to update the president on where we are, and I don't think I have anything to actually update him on. I'm still not sure we're not chasing a ghost. The Chinese getting one up on us is nothing new. While we were busy fighting terrorists, they've been hard at work strengthening their position. Snatching up all sorts of strategic ports and infrastructure through their One Belt One Road program, sucking unsuspecting countries into predatory loan agreements, and engaging in intellectual-property theft on a scale the average American couldn't even fathom. Maybe we are just straight-up being outplayed. Either way, the president wants answers and he wants options. His whole election campaign centered around regaining American strength, and he can't afford to continue looking weak against our main competitor now."

"Is that what you think? If so, then why did you sign off on us going into the Philippines?" Colonel Banks asked.

"We've worked together for too long, Jason. Whenever you bring something up to me, I know better than to doubt your intuition. You've always had that ability to pick out that thing no one else sees. So, tell me, what's your sense of things now? Is there something here?"

"Sir, it's at least enough to keep this team digging."

"Thanks, Jason. Let me know if they find anything." Cantrell stood and walked out of the room.

Matt stood quietly and watched as Colonel Banks talked with a few of the general's staff. After a few minutes the room had cleared out.

"Matt, none of that was about you," Colonel Banks said once they were alone. "General Cantrell is in a political knife fight right now over funding. DOD is taking huge budget cuts now that Iraq and Afghanistan are over. Since we've changed from focusing on countering insurgencies and terrorist organizations to fighting major conflicts, the Pentagon sees SOCOM as a prime target to absorb most of the budget cuts. The logic being that we need more tanks and fighter aircraft than special operations forces, so the service chiefs jump at any opportunity to score points at our expense."

"They would rather have one more F-35 than actually understand the fight they're getting themselves into? That doesn't make much sense."

"It does if you're playing their game. Just be thankful you're not."

"I'd rather permanently move in to SERE school than have to deal with that."

"Stick around long enough, Matt, and you'll end up there. That's the path of an officer. You don't get to stay tactical for long. Better enjoy it while you can."

"So what's the plan, sir?"

"We keep chasing the rabbit. I'll stick the analysts back on the problem and see what they drag up. In the meantime, what'd you do with the piece you brought home with you?"

"I've still got it."

"A guy I went to the War College with works as a project manager at DARPA building new computers or something. He might be able to point you in the right direction. I'll dig up his contact info from my email on the ride back to headquarters."

Matt navigated the late-morning traffic through the beltway in silence while Colonel Banks sat in the passenger seat checking emails on his laptop. When you're the commander of one of the most elite special-operations units in the entire country, the things demanding your attention are unending. Although the command position could be a possibility for Matt down the road, he wasn't sure he wanted it. Sure, it came with the ability to influence national security and foreign policy, but the thought of being tied up in meetings all day and chained to email in between didn't appeal to him. He hadn't really known what being an officer meant when the recruiter talked him into joining ROTC, but he'd worked hard throughout his career to avoid the stereotypical office-dwelling fate of his peers and the politics that inevitably went with it.

As Matt pulled up to the front of the unit headquarters,

Colonel Banks took an index card from his pocket and wrote a name and address before handing it to Matt.

"Here's the info for Oliver Nascent. I shot him a note, so he's expecting you. Let me know what you find." Colonel Banks shut the lid on his laptop, got out of the car, and headed for the entrance to the headquarters. Matt watched as the door closed behind the colonel and then entered the address into his GPS.

Chapter 3

"Two weeks. I lasted two weeks out of college before my first firing." Drew said as she sat down across from Ish. Beginning on the first day of their internships, the two had quickly claimed this table at the building's small coffee shop for their morning breaks.

"Good morning, Ish. Nice to see you, Ish," he said, looking up from his phone.

"This is no time for pleasantries. What am I going to do?"

"TurboTax," Ish laughed.

"You're not helping."

"And you're blowing this out of proportion. You weren't fired. The powers that be simply decided that herbivore robots weren't cool enough to keep funding. It's like the cybernetic version of natural selection: survival of the fittest. Or the most interesting."

"Still sucks. On the plus side, though, my team lead said that I could pick another machine-learning project based out of this campus to join since this one is now defunct, and she would get me on it."

"See. Silver lining. Any ideas on where you might want to go?"

"Yeah, I want to move onto Skynet with you. That was the

plan when we first applied, right? To get onto the same project together. Do you think I have a snowball's chance in hell of that happening?"

"I don't know if they're looking for more people. To be honest, I'm not sure how much longer this project is going to be active either. As close as we are to completion, rumor is that we might be up on the chopping block too," Ish said.

"Don't you want to work together though? It would be just like we're back at Tech."

"Of course I do. That's not what I meant. I just mean . . . Never mind, I don't know what I mean. If you want, when we go back upstairs I can introduce you to Rich, our project lead, to get the ball rolling on getting you on board."

"That would be perfect. Thank you."

Drew and Ish sat in silence drinking their coffee and scrolling through their various social media accounts, each occasionally reaching over to show the other a particularly funny meme or interesting post. After finishing her cup and noticing Ish was also done, Drew got up.

"Shall we?" she asked.

"Let's do it," Ish stood up and threw his empty paper cup into the recycling.

The two made their way out of the coffee shop back toward the elevators. Drew pushed the call button and stood back next to Ish.

"So how did things go with your Tinder hookup last night?" Drew asked.

"What are you talking about?"

"I heard you leave at like eleven thirty last night. My guess is that you weren't going to the library, so I'm assuming you went out to meet up with some chick you met online. How'd it go?"

Ish looked at Drew uneasily, and his face flushed.

"Dude, there's no shame in that game. You do you. I just hope you'll find one worth bringing around before too long. I need more girl friends in my life," Drew said.

"Oh yeah, well, it's nothing. Nothing happened. You know how I am. Stereotypical nerd—all thumbs with the lady folk," Ish offered as the elevator doors parted.

Drew leaned over to make another comment, but decided against it after seeing how uncomfortable Ish had become. When the elevators opened, Ish rushed out only to immediately run into the back of someone.

"Oh, crap. I'm so sorry," Ish said.

Matt turned around. "No harm, no foul," he said. "Do you work here? I'm trying to find Oliver Nascent's office. The directory in the lobby has his office listed as 308, but it's empty."

"No, sorry," Ish said. "We've only been here for a couple of weeks. 308 was a nanotechnology team, though, and I think their office space got moved to the fifth floor when they consolidated several of the machine-learning projects here."

"Oh, thanks," Matt said. "So you two are working on artificial-intelligence programs?"

"Someone has to usher in the next stage of human civilization, right?" Drew said.

"That's really cool. I'll check out the fifth floor. Thanks for the tip," Matt said. "Don't build anything evil," he added through the closing elevator doors.

"Smooth, Ish," Drew said, turning toward her friend.

"Stuff it," Ish said as he started down the hallway.

Drew caught up with him and the pair walked toward the office at the end of the hall.

Ish knocked on the office's door frame. "Rich, do you have a minute?"

"Sure, Ish. Come in," Rich said, coming from behind the desk to greet them. "What's up?"

"Rich, I wanted to introduce you to Drew. She and I went to school together before getting picked up for internships here. She seems to have drawn the short straw, and was assigned to a project that was just shut down. Do we have space to slide her onto our project?"

"Great to meet you, Drew. Have a seat, and we'll see what we can find." Rich motioned toward a brown leather couch occupying the entire wall opposite his desk and sat back down in his office chair. Drew and Ish sat on the couch.

"Let's see," Rich mumbled to himself as he did something on his computer. "Here we go—packets for this year's interns." He opened the file and began scrolling through the documents until he found the one he was looking for. "Andrea Drum. Graduated Virginia Tech, 3.8 GPA, computer science with a concentration in machine learning . . . looks like on paper you've ticked the right boxes. Why do you want to join the Advanced Operational Decision-Making Project?"

"To be honest," Drew said, "mostly because Ish is here. More than that, though, he told me a little bit about what he's been doing, and it sounds really interesting. A system that can take in the ridiculous amount of data coming off of a modern battlefield and return the best course of action would be incredible. If we have to go to war, I think I would want something like that helping our generals."

Rich nodded. "It would be something. Especially once we can house it in a system with the computational horsepower it needs. Then it's just a matter of feeding it data. The more data, the better it works. I think we should be able to find a spot for you. Ish, can you get her set up at an empty workstation? I'll send a note to Cynthia to add you to all of the relevant teams. Welcome aboard."

-

The elevator door opened and Matt exited into the hallway of the fifth floor. Although he thought it was likely futile, he checked to see if the floor's directory board had been updated. Reaching the bottom of the list and confirming his suspicion, Matt walked down the hallway, its dingy tile floor reminiscent of every other government building he'd been in, looking for open doors and people inside who could point him in the right direction. Four open offices and two short conversations later, Matt knocked on a door two-thirds of the way down, stepping back once he heard the sound of footsteps from within.

"Can I help you?" a bald man in his late fifties asked as the door swung open.

"Sorry to bother you," Matt replied, "I'm looking for Dr. Oliver Nascent."

"Well, you've found him. What can I do for you?"

"Dr. Nascent, my name is Matt Anderson. Jason Banks gave me your name as someone who might be able to help me identify something."

"Oh, right. JB mentioned someone was going to come by. Come in, come in." The man turned back into the small room. As Dr. Nascent moved away from the door, Matt could see that nearly every available space was covered with stacks of books, journals, and papers. He watched as the scientist scanned the space, came to a decision, and removed a stack of journals from one of the chairs. "Have a seat."

"Thank you," Matt said as he walked into the room, trying not to knock anything over. "I was hoping you could tell me about this thing I came across recently." Reaching into his bag, Matt removed the dull black chunk and passed it across the desk.

"Huh," Dr. Nascent grunted as he took the object and turned it over in his hand. "What can you tell me about it?" Something in the tone of the scientist's question let Matt know that this was not the first time he had been shown something pulled off of a classified mission, and that, unlike most scientists, he would accept anything that Matt said or didn't say about the thing and where it came from.

"Honestly, I don't really know much. I came across a system physically installed in a server room. When I opened it up, this was attached in the center of a circuit board. The rest of the components were in worse shape than this, but looked like normal electronic components to me. There was something about this, though, that stood out."

"Interesting. Any idea what caused this?"

"There was no sign of anything around it catching fire, so most likely the device itself catastrophically failed. Whoever designed it knew it would have heat issues, though, because the device came with strict instructions about additional fans for cooling. There were also direct threats warning the server admins against unplugging the device for any reason. It's almost like they knew this might happen."

Dr. Nascent set the device down on the desk and leaned back, staring at it. After a minute, he slapped the armrests of his chair and stood up. "Follow me," he said, walking out of the office with the device in his hand. Matt followed him to a lab at the end of the hall. Dr. Nascent walked to a device, resting on a table, that looked similar to a small refrigerator. Opening the door, he placed the device inside before sitting on a stool in front of a computer monitor. The scientist entered a series of commands before striking the Enter key with a flourish. After a few moments, the screen changed to display a series of colored graphs with a wall of text beside it. For the next five minutes, Matt watched as Dr. Nascent scrolled up and down the data readouts, making sense of what he saw.

Opening the container and removing the device, Dr. Nascent turned back to Matt. "Do you need this device to stay in this condition, or can I . . . take some small liberties with it?"

"It's pretty well destroyed, so if you think it would help, then go ahead."

Dr. Nascent took a knife from a nearby drawer, removed slivers from three different places on the surface of the device, and used a drill to collect a sample from the center. He repeated the same routine with the computer for each of the four individual pieces, each time scrolling up and down the data readouts.

"And now let's take a peek and see what these look like," he said, rolling over to a microscope on a nearby table. Again, Dr. Nascent examined each sample in turn. Frowning, he got up and, without a word, walked out of the lab. Matt grabbed the device and the four samples, followed him back down to the office, and sat back down to watch as Dr. Nascent began scrolling through files. After a few minutes, the scientist got up and walked to a pile of papers on a stool in the corner and began thumbing through them. Finally, he pulled a printed journal article from the stack and handed it to Matt.

"You need to talk with Lee Chen," he said with a sense of finality that made Matt fairly sure he had missed a complete conversation the man had just carried on in his own head.

"Who?" Matt asked. Looking down at the stapled papers in his hand, he saw that the lead author was an L. Chen.

"Dr. Lee Chen is a researcher out of Cal Tech. He's done a lot of work on advanced-computer-system design. Super interesting stuff."

"What did you find?"

"What I found doesn't make any sense. Actually, two things don't make any sense." Picking up one of the samples off the desk, Dr. Nascent continued. "This is mostly copper. Do you see those ripples on the top of the device right there? This is from that. Those ripples were likely once fins that worked to dissipate heat. Most electronics have them, and a lot of higher-end stuff uses copper instead of aluminum. Even though it's more expensive, it works better. This isn't all copper, though. It's an alloy with a bunch of other things in it. Elements that are hard to find and harder to work with. Whoever designed this system was clearly obsessed with heat dissipation."

"Not that it ended up doing them much good," Matt added.

"That's just it. Why would someone spend so much effort designing these heat sinks but then field the system before it was tested enough to identify conditions for such catastrophic failure? And why wouldn't they swap to using a cryogenic cooling system? That doesn't make sense. It's more plausible that they couldn't go with something as massive as a cryogenic cooler, and this was the best alternative they could engineer based on some other operating constraints. They likely knew that this was ultimately a doomed setup, and went with it anyway, knowing that the system would eventually fail."

"Why wouldn't they put in a fail-safe where it just turned off when it got too hot? Lots of systems have that."

"Again, design choice. Maybe it was worth being a single-use device. Maybe once it was turned on it couldn't be shut down. We have a lot of assumptions, and not a lot of answers with that one."

"What about the second thing you mentioned?"

"That's why you have to go talk to Lee. I have no idea what's going on with the rest of the device. It's mostly neodymium, which has been used in electronics for years. Never in the quantity in that device compared to everything else, though. A few years ago Lee wrote that paper I handed you, stating that a theoretical neodymium mesh could be one of the key breakthroughs we would need for the next generation of supercomputers. It received a bunch of push back from the academy, though, with a couple people rage-publishing about how it was impossible."

"But you think that this might be that?"

"I think I have no idea. That's why you need to go talk with him. Sorry I don't have all the answers."

"No, don't be. Thank you so much for your time."

"I still owe JB for helping me get through the War College. Never was one for the strategy stuff. People are too messy. It's the least I can do."

Walking out to his car, Matt pulled out his phone and booked a flight to LAX.

Chapter 4

"Mr. President! Mr. President!" fifty reporters all shouted over one another, vying for the opportunity to ask questions of the chief executive after his prepared remarks concluded. President Jack Sanderson ignored all of them and called on a reporter his staffers had probably selected in advance.

"Mr. President, aren't you worried that these new tariffs will drive the wedge between the US and China even further? What do you say to the rumors that these tariffs are nothing more than an attempt for this administration to save face after the disaster at the Southeast Asian Trade Summit?"

"I would say that my record to date speaks for itself. Everything that I have done—every policy I've enacted, every action I have taken—since assuming this office has been fair and with an eye towards what is best for this country. I have never stooped to playing vindictive, petty games of tit for tat, and I am not about to start now. Frankly, this new policy is bigger than just the United States. It is about free trade and freedom of choice for the entire world."

President Sanderson paused to let the last phrase linger.

"We are not the world police, as some administrations have acted in the past, but we are a member of the global community. And as good neighbors who find ourselves in a position to help, I feel compelled to act. For years, we have watched as Chinese expansion through policies like its One Belt One Road initiative have preyed on developing nations around the world. Although China came under the auspices of peace with promises of joint prosperity, those nations who welcomed it as a friend quickly found that they had let in a wolf. They learned that these policies were not about a rising tide raising all boats, but about extracting anything of value for use in China for the betterment of the Chinese alone. This is happening all over the world. Any nation who has precious natural resources that China needs to feed its insatiable appetite is feeling the pressure.

"The word is out, however, as world leaders are beginning to see what these deals really mean for them and their people. Leaders like Vietnamese Prime Minister Pham Van Dong, who stepped away from the negotiating table with their northern neighbor because he refused to sell out his country's future for an easy payday. But they cannot do it alone. They need support from the rest of us to stand up for what is right. And that is what we are doing. We are standing up with our friends and allies around the world to say unequivocally that we will not sit silently and watch as one country tramples on everything we have fought to build for their own selfish gains. Next question."

Matt poked the power button on the screen affixed to the seat in front of him and sat back, looking out the window. He wasn't sure how much of the president's speech was true and how much was spin. While he made valid points, Sanderson hated to lose, and given the opportunity to stick it to an opponent, Matt guessed that he wouldn't think too hard before taking it.

In Matt's meeting with General Cantrell, the SOCOM

commander had mentioned a meeting with the president. It made sense that Cantrell was so upset at the lack of clarity about what was going on the Philippines if he was about to walk into a room where Sanderson would make a decision on how to respond to the Chinese. *We're still three steps behind on this thing*, Matt thought. And then something struck him. He had just used *we* to refer to both himself and the most senior leaders in the country, and not in a vague, general way. For the first time in his career, he clearly saw the connection between what he was doing—his mission—and the decisions coming out of the White House. When he had first applied to join the unit, Matt had been searching for a way to make a bigger impact. He now saw he'd been given exactly that—if he could figure out what this thing was and what the Chinese were doing with it. In a few hours, he would land in Los Angeles. Hopefully the trip would be worth it, and Dr. Chen would have some of the answers he was after.

-

Matt set his bag down in the passenger seat of the rental car and pulled up the GPS on his phone. One hour, it told him, with only minor traffic. As he pulled out of the parking garage, Matt wondered if he would be that lucky. Staring at an unending wall of brake lights that greeted him on the highway, he watched the arrival estimator on his GPS creep later and later. An hour later than initially expected, Matt pulled into a parking spot on Cal Tech's campus and stepped out into the warm afternoon sun. The sidewalks were full of students making their way between classes, and seeing them made Matt nostalgic for his own time in college. The weather was better in Pasadena than Knoxville, though.

He found the building that housed most of the computer-engineering faculty, and walked up to the side entrance. As he reached for the handle, the door flew outward, forcing Matt to jump back out of the way as a student in a gray hoodie sprinted past him. *Guess he forgot to set an alarm*, Matt thought as he climbed the stairs to the second floor. Walking down the hallway, he watched the numbers on the offices slowly descend until he found the one he was looking for. Although the door was partially open, Matt knocked out of courtesy.

"Dr. Chen?" he called out, knocking again.

Not hearing a reply, Matt slowly opened the door. "Dr. Che—" He stopped mid sentence as he saw a man slumped over the desk. Blood covered most of the desk's surface and was dripping off the edge onto the carpet below. Matt rushed over, but as soon as he got close, he could tell that there was nothing to be done for the man. His throat had been cut. Matt touched the man's cheek with the back of his hand while he looked over the scene. Realizing that this was likely no more than a few minutes old, he ran out of the office to the end of the hallway. He looked out the window, trying to spot the student in the hoodie who had rushed past him, but whoever that was was long gone.

Matt strode back down the hall and into the office. He knew he didn't have long before someone else would walk by, and he didn't want to get tangled up in this mess. He pulled out a pair of latex gloves and slipped them on as he began taking in the room. On the wall hung several framed diplomas granting various degrees to Lee Chen, confirming this was the guy Matt had been trying to find. Next, Matt looked on the desk for a computer. Moving around behind the still-occupied desk chair, he felt something under his foot. He bent down and picked up a laptop. It rattled in his hands, and when he flipped the computer over, he saw several large puncture marks in the case. Unsure if it had hit the hard drive or not, Matt slid the computer into his bag. His attention then moved back onto the desk next to the keyboard where Chen's wallet sat. Matt picked it up. Money, credit cards, IDs all still there. Whoever had done this hadn't even bothered to make it look like a botched robbery. Matt took a photo of the driver's license along with a couple other photos of the room. Checking that the hallway was clear, he slid out of the office and cracked the door behind him.

He made his way back to the parking garage and sat in his car, trying to figure out his next move. Any moment, someone would stumble across Dr. Chen's body. From there, the police would be swarming all over the office, followed closely by the scientist's house, lab, and any other location easily linked to him as they tried to piece together the homicide case. Unsure how to identify what lab space belonged to the late scientist or if he wanted to risk being seen poking around campus more, Matt decided that his chances of finding additional information about who had killed Dr. Chen and why were better if he visited the scientist's home. Pulling his phone from his pocket, Matt scrolled to the photo of Chen's driver's license and typed the address into his GPS. Eight minutes. At least the professor lived close by.

Matt drove down the small residential street and passed the address listed on Chen's license. No cars were in the driveway, and none of the lights were on despite dusk fast approaching. Matt turned the corner at the end of the block and parked along a narrow side street. Sliding his bag across his shoulder, he walked along the row of houses and then up the driveway alongside Chen's residence. After the first couple of feet, the property was well screened from the surrounding neighborhood by a thick hedge, so the chance of being spotted by a neighbor dropped dramatically as he rounded the corner to the back of the house. Climbing the three wooden steps onto the back porch, Matt reached out for the doorknob and froze. The windowpane above the handle was broken, and the door was not closed fully.

Straining to listen for any sounds of movement in the house, Matt was fairly certain that there was at least one person inside. Given that the door was ajar and the lights were off, he was pretty sure whoever was in the house wasn't an invited guest. Cautiously, he pushed the door open just enough to slip into the kitchen. Now fully inside, he could hear someone moving around in an adjacent room on this floor. Instinctively, Matt reached for his pistol, and then cursed himself when he remembered that the Glock wasn't there. He was on US soil. There had seemed to be no need to worry about getting a firearm through the airport to go have a conversation with a college professor. Looking around, he found the knife block next to the stove and drew out a carving knife.

Matt crept through the kitchen toward the open entrance to the next room, stopping just short of the threshold. The movement he had heard a moment ago had stopped, and he paused trying to locate the intruder in the next room. Steeling himself to move around the corner, Matt gripped the knife in his hand. As he moved through the doorway, he caught a glimpse of the butt of a pistol, but it was too late. The weapon struck home in the center of his forehead, and he crumpled to the floor.

Opening his eyes, Matt strained to see through the blur of pain ringing in his head. He lay motionless, listening for any sign of his attacker, but heard nothing. Matt slowly stood up and got his bearings as the blur slowly began to fade. As it did, he began to realize just how lucky he had been. Whoever he had encountered clearly had no issues killing people, and if they had wanted Matt dead there was nothing he could have done to stop them. Pushing that unsettling thought aside, he tried to focus on the immediate task at hand. First, he checked the rest of the rooms to make sure he was alone and to get a sense for how the house was laid out. Finding nothing of interest, he returned to the office.

Papers and books littered the floor, along with the contents of most of the desk drawers. It looked like whoever this person was had finished their search. Since none of the rest of the house was disturbed, Matt concluded that the intruder either had found what they'd been after, or hadn't but had decided that it was unlikely to be anywhere else in the house. Either way, it wasn't worth the time to search through everything again when he didn't even know what he was looking for. Especially since the police were eventually going to be knocking on the dead man's door. Taking photos of the room, Matt stopped at the desk, looking down at the laptop. It had received the same violent treatment as the one in Chen's office. Still, Matt thought, there might be some way to salvage the data. Sliding it into his bag next to the other punctured computer, he retraced his steps through the back door. Out on the street once more, Matt returned to his car and drove out of the neighborhood as quickly as he could without drawing attention to himself. As he turned onto the highway, he passed two patrol cars heading in the direction of the house.

Having lost his lead to understanding what the device was and linked himself to two active crime scenes, Matt decided that he shouldn't linger in Los Angeles any longer. Matt drove to the airport and booked a seat on the next flight out to Dulles. He spent the remainder of the drive thinking about how he was going to explain to the colonel what had happened. Banks would not be happy.

Chapter 5

"Henry, Randy, Beth, and I are going out for a drink. You in?" Drew asked, leaning against Ish's desk.

"You sure have made friends around here really quickly," Ish replied without looking up from his keyboard.

"Yeah, well, what can I say? I'm popular among a certain crowd."

"A group that would also identify as Battlestar Galactica superfans."

"You know you're a representative element of both of those groups, right? Which would make that a self-burn more than anything else."

"Guilty, I suppose. I think I'll have to pass. I want to finish this up before I close out for the weekend."

"Suit yourself. I'm not sure exactly where Beth said she wanted to go, so if you change your mind, shoot me a text and I'll drop a pin wherever we end up." Pushing up off the desk, Drew left Ish to finish his work.

"Drew, let's go!" Henry shouted from the end of the hall.

"I'm coming, I'm coming. I was just trying to get Ish the Party Destroyer to come with us," she replied. No sooner had she stopped next to her colleagues than the elevator chimed open and the four shuffled inside.

"Ish isn't coming?" Randy asked as the door closed.

"No, he said he wanted to stick around for a bit to finish up some things," Drew said.

"Seems like he's making a habit of that," Henry observed. "Trying to make a good impression, huh?"

"I've never been quite sure if people who work late are really that much more dedicated and productive or if they are just terrible at time management," Beth said.

"Well, if the newbie doesn't figure out how to relax, he's going to burn himself out," Randy said.

"You've been in government your entire career. You know nothing about burning anything out," Henry poked at his colleague. "But now it's Friday, and we've had a hell of a good week. Time for a drink."

With everyone in agreement, they walked out into the evening air.

"You've picked up on our project quickly, Drew," Beth said, pacing alongside the younger woman. "It's been fun watching you weave your way through the model and figure out what we've got. Plus, it's been nice having another woman on the team."

"I mean, I am a little disappointed about the lack of kelp," Drew replied with a smile. "I am really happy to be here, though. I spent so much time in school working on projects that were just beginning, so it's been really great getting to pick up on the tail end for a change. I mean, this system is pretty much ready for field trials."

"It is exciting, right? I'm not sure if we will actually get to play with real units. I know there was talk about hopping onto a training exercise at one of the big bases out in the desert, but I wouldn't be surprised if that gets shot down. Army commanders tend to be suspicious of artificial intelligence, and with good reason," Beth said as she opened the bar door. "After you."

"Thank you, ma'am." Drew grinned and walked inside the bar. "What do you want? I've got the first one. I'm going for an orange crush. I went to a place in Annapolis over the weekend that had those, and they are now officially my favorite drink."

"With a review like that, how could I not go with one of those? Looks like Henry's found us a table. I'll meet you over there in a second," Beth said, walking toward the restroom.

Drew edged up to the bar and ordered the two drinks. Waiting for the bartender to complete her order, she slowly became aware of a sense of happiness. Not that she wasn't a generally happy person, but this felt different somehow-deeper. As she stared at her reflection in the mirror behind the bar, she realized she was content. This is what she wanted—what she had been working toward the last four years. She had a job she found interesting that might actually do some good in the world. She was exploring a new city and living with her best friend. And now she had work friends who did work-friend things like get drinks on a Friday.

"Here you go," the bartender said as he slid the glasses toward Drew. "Do you want to start a tab?"

"That would be great." Reaching into her pocket, Drew realized that she had left her phone and wallet on her desk in her rush to catch up with the rest of the team. "Oh crap, I forgot my wallet. I'll be right back."

Drew sheepishly walked over to the table where Henry and Randy were talking over a couple of beers. "Ah, guys, I left my wallet back in the office."

"Well, isn't that convenient!" Randy laughed. "No problem.

I've got a tab open. Tell him to just put everything on mine, and we can settle up whenever."

"Thanks," Drew said. "I can't believe I did that."

Returning to the table a couple minutes later, Drew sat down and pushed one of the drinks over to Beth.

"Thanks, Randy," she said.

"No problem. I'm a little surprised he didn't check your ID. Must have been into you," Randy replied.

"Um, he actually said he was into you. So I gave him your number," Drew shot back.

Randy blushed and stared at her silently for a few moments until Henry burst into laughter. "You should see the look of horror on your face, Randy!" he howled. "Oh man, I'm glad you're on the team, Drew."

Drew sipped her drink in triumph, and then turned back to Beth. "You were saying that you don't think that the Army is going to want to use our system? Why is that?"

"Because they don't understand it and it scares the crap out of them."

"So then why is the DOD investing money into developing a system they won't even use?"

"It's not that they won't use it. It's that they don't trust it right now. Defense innovation is a weird space. There is a constant game of one-upmanship where everyone is constantly trying to build bigger, better weapons that will give them an advantage in the next conflict. That's all well and good when a project is just an upgrade on previous tools. A new and improved rifle is still just a rifle. It may be more accurate or shoot better bullets, but it's still essentially the same thing. When something really new comes along, though, like the airplane, the guys at the top really don't know how to use it, or how they should change the way they fight to take advantage of the new technology. So they have to guess, and there is a potentially catastrophic downside if they guess wrong: they lose the next war. So the generals are stuck in this position where they constantly have to create new technology, but then are very slow to actually change how they wage war. At least in peacetime. Once the war starts, all bets are off and it's a race for everyone to adapt to whatever new tools and strategies prove to be the most effective. Like ditching battleships in favor of aircraft carriers during the Second World War."

"And you know all this as a computer engineer because . . ." Drew asked.

"Because before I went to school and got my fancy degrees, I was in the Navy for six years and lived on one of those carriers. But AI is even more scary to the brass, because it threatens to replace them. The system we've created can take in so much more data and crunch the numbers so much faster than they can. It can sense what is happening on the battlefield, analyze the situation, find a solution, and execute a response in the time it would take a human commander to even listen to a single intelligence report. They don't want to be replaced, so it's a little bit of a job-security thing. The other problem they have is with ethics. They are afraid that if they let the machines make the decisions, it will go full Machiavelli on them and commit all sorts of heinous acts that go against our ideas of morality and how wars should be fought."

"You make it sound like they're making a deal with the devil," Drew said, placing her empty glass on the table.

"Well, that is kind of how they see it, but since everyone else is rushing to build these systems, they don't feel like they can afford to miss out. Which is why we've built our mechanical

Napoleon, but we may not get to see it in action."

"Still weird to me," Drew said. "I'm starving." She looked at the rest of the group. "Are you guys up for getting food somewhere?"

"Nah, Julie is expecting me home soon," Randy replied.

"I'm out too," Beth said. "I'll have a furry riot on my hands if I don't get home to feed the cat before too long. I ran out of her food this morning, so I need to go pick some up."

"Well, these two losers say no, but I would love some Thai," Henry offered.

"I could do some pad thai. From the place just down from the office?" Drew asked.

"Works for me."

"OK. I have to run back up there anyway to grab my phone. How about I meet you there?"

"Sold. I'll grab a booth and now that these two are gone we can finally talk about them behind their backs," Henry said, pointing at Beth and Randy.

Drew walked along the sidewalk, retracing her steps back to the office. Rounding the corner to the front entrance, she saw Ish crossing the street on the far side of the building. *Great,* she thought, *maybe Ish wants to come to dinner.* She picked up her pace to catch up with him, but before she could get close enough to call out to him, he got into the back of a black SUV that had been parked on the corner. A man closed the door behind him and climbed into the driver's seat. Drew watched as the car drove away. *Why would Ish take a fancy Uber?* she asked herself. *We live like six blocks from here.* Shrugging at her own question, Drew walked back to the double doors to the building to get her phone.

-

Frank slid the headphones over his ears and clicked Connect. The message from the operations officer back stateside had been a little light on details since it was sent through an unsecured commercial line, so he wasn't sure exactly what sort of meeting he was joining. The teleconference window popped up on his computer, and Frank saw the First Special Forces Group conference room displayed on the other end.

"Frank, this is Major Davis, how do you have me?" came a voice from the distant end.

"I've got you good on audio and video, sir. How me?" Frank replied.

"I've got you the same. The commander will be in here shortly." Major Davis came into view with the conference room's remote control in his hand and sat down in one of the seats near the head of the table. Looking at the other faces in the room, Frank recognized his battalion commander, the battalion's command sergeant major, the group intelligence officer, and a couple other people Frank had seen around the compound but had never met. A few moments later, the door to the conference room opened, and the group commander, Colonel Vorhees, walked in.

"Frank, how are you? How's the training going?" Colonel Vorhees asked as he sat down.

"Hey, sir. We're all doing well out here. We're done with squad live fire, and have been running some of the platoons through some patrolling exercises. So far everything is going really well. The Vietnamese Rangers are squared away, and it's been fun working with them. They've even shown Rizzo a few tricks for navigating in the really thick jungle."

"Glad to hear it. How's Kathy?"

Frank smiled at the sound of his wife's name. Colonel Vorhees and his wife had hosted a dinner for the new officers when Frank had arrived. Kathy and Rebecca Vorhees had connected and become close friends over the past year. Although the social connection with the group commander made him feel awkward, he was surprised at how happy it made him now. "She's good, sir. Just trying to stay one step ahead of our three-year-old."

"If she's even got a full step ahead of a toddler by herself, she's doing all right. So Frank, here's the deal. I've got to call an audible on you and change up your plans a little bit. I got a call from SOCPAC last night. Admiral Jennings is asking for some support."

"Sir, if a Navy SEAL, who also happens to be in charge of all of the special operations forces in the Pacific, is asking a Green Beret for help, something must be up. How can I help?" Frank asked, realizing that this was more than just a routine check-in.

"We've been getting reports of some activity along the Vietnamese-Chinese border. Our attaché in Hanoi went over to the MOD and met with their defense minister this morning. They asked for some support with intelligence and threat analysis. When he mentioned that we had an ODA already in-country training with their Rangers, the minister said he would like to send them up north with you in an advise-and-assist capacity to see what was going on. For a little bit more background, I'll turn it over to the S2 and his intel analysts. Take it away, Jim."

"Thanks, sir," the group's intelligence officer picked up the conversation. "Last month, economic talks between Vietnam and China broke down. The Chinese had been trying to broker a deal for rights to some newly discovered deposits of rare-earth minerals north of Hanoi. The Vietnamese government came into the talks already agitated by the continual aggressive activities of the Chinese fishing fleets and land-reclamation projects in the South China Sea that have been encroaching into Vietnam's economic-exclusion zone and starting to get dangerously close to their territorial waters. It looks like the Chinese came in with their normal One Belt One Road strategies, but Vietnam shut them down pretty hard.

"A week later, the Vietnamese intelligence service found out that China's next move was to simply buy the largest mining firm in the country through a shell corporation. Through some emergency legislation, Vietnam blocked the acquisition and escalated the war of words. China has responded in kind through its propaganda machine, and has started leveling all sorts of accusations at the Vietnamese government. We've also seen some attempts to influence public opinion in their favor within the country. They've also upped the frequency and scale of their intimidation tactics—low-level flybys with fighters, close calls with naval vessels, things like that. None of that really bothers me, though. It all feels like a normal day at the office for international competition with the Chinese these days. Economic and informational warfare with a mixture of some bully posturing for good measure.

"What is concerning, though, is what is quietly happening along the border. We've had a mixture of human source reporting, signals intelligence, and overhead imagery from satellites of some low-level infiltrations by the Chinese. Small teams of three or four coming across the border possibly doing some reconnaissance. We've been able to confirm four of these within the last week scattered across the border. There's not much in the way of sensing up there since it's pretty remote, so we don't know what their objective is. They do seem to be trying to keep a low profile, though, so it's unlikely that these incursions are a part of the intimidation campaign. My imagery analyst has laid out this activity into a document which should be in your inbox now, Frank. Pending any questions, sir, that's all I have."

"Thanks, Jim," Colonel Vorhees picked up. "So, Frank, that's what we've got. What I'd like is for you to take your team and go with the Ranger company up north and see if you can't figure out what's going on up there. Don't go up there and start a land war in Asia, but we need some answers. I can't think of anybody better suited to the task than an ODA of Green Berets and a well-trained partner force. Any equipment or logistics requirements you identify during your planning, we'll send your way, and we'll feed you more information as we receive it. Just don't waste time getting up there."

"Yes, sir. I think I've got it. I'm sure we'll have some questions as we work through our plan, but we'll route those back through ops channels. We'll go see what they're up to."

"That's it." Colonel Vorhees ended the session, and Frank's screen turned black.

"Holy crap," Frank said as he took off his headset. "Rizzo, grab the team. We've got stuff to do."

When the twelve men had gathered in the small office they had taken over as a team room during this trip, Frank filled them in on the meeting and their assignment. For the next few hours, the team pored over the images the analysts had sent and devised an initial plan and a list of the equipment and support they would need for the change in mission.

Once they understood their next steps, Frank went to find Lieutenant Nguyen, along with Mac, in case he needed some help translating. Meanwhile, Rizzo sat down behind the secure laptop and began making phone calls to coordinate for the things they needed.

"Good afternoon, Captain," Lieutenant Nguyen said as he rose from his desk to shake Frank's hand.

"How are we doing, Lieutenant?"

"I'm afraid that I've been better. My commander just ordered me back to headquarters saying that I am no longer a part of this exercise. This is a disappointment, as I have been learning a lot."

"That's what I came to talk to you about. My guess is that you're about to have the same conversation with your commander that I just got done having with mine." Lieutenant Nguyen looked confused, so Frank continued. "I don't want to get ahead of your boss, but it looks like we have been assigned to do some reconnaissance up north. There are some intel reports that are a little concerning, and the powers that be want us to go take a look. Come get me when you get back from your headquarters and we'll figure out what we're doing."

Frank could see the lieutenant's demeanor change as he realized the implications of what Frank had just said. "I will. Thank you. Training is over, and now it's time to put our skills to use."

"Exactly, my friend. See you when you get back," Frank said as he left the lieutenant's office.

-

Matt walked out of Colonel Banks's office and through the

command suite. For having learned that one of his operatives had almost been killed, the commander was much calmer than Matt had expected. There was no way Matt could have reasonably expected that going to visit a professor about some paper the man had written five years ago would put him in the situation to find a body and end up unconscious on the man's floor, but still he'd figured Colonel Banks would be more upset. Matt guessed that this was not the first time the unit commander had dealt with worse problems than this and was glad that Colonel Banks wasn't going to lecture him on his inexperience.

He was also glad that the colonel's parting words had been to "lie low for a while" and not "drop this thing immediately," which Matt interpreted as an implicit statement to keep digging into what, if anything, connected Dr. Chen's murder and the Philippines device. It couldn't be a coincidence that shortly after the Chinese had run into him and Jacob snooping around their new device, they had assassinated a professor working on advanced-computer design. But what the connection was still eluded him. Unfortunately, Matt was now left with only two broken computers to find some answers. He may have neglected to mention them in his debrief to the colonel, but he would turn them over to the civilian criminal investigators once he had a chance to see if there was anything of value he could get out of them. Speaking of, he might as well go talk to the unit's FBI liaison now and get that over with.

"Got a second, Greg?" Matt asked, standing in the doorway to a small office off on the operations floor.

"Sure, come on in," Greg replied.

Moving into the room and extending his hand, Matt introduced himself. "Matt Anderson, great to meet you. I'm in A Squadron."

"Pleasure to meet you, Matt," Greg said, shaking Matt's hand. "What's up?"

"The boss told me to come down and talk to you about an incident that happened yesterday out in LA. A professor I went out to talk to about a project I'm working wound up dead. His office and home were ransacked, and I had a run-in with whoever did this at the guy's house."

"Ah, OK," Greg said, "Not my favorite part of me being here, but acting as an intermediary between law enforcement and unit operatives in mission-related situations is part of the job. Fill me in on the details, and I'll reach out to the LAPD. We'll probably have a couple more follow-on conversations as they work through their investigation, but as long as everything is legit, we shouldn't have to link you back to the situation."

As Greg took notes, Matt recounted his trip to Los Angeles and the events that had unfolded. After some back-and-forth in which Greg posed clarifying questions the LAPD investigators were likely to ask, the two ended the conversation the FBI veteran stood up. "I think I've got what I need. I'll circle back with you if anything comes back on this," Greg said, extending his hand.

Matt shook Greg's hand. "Thanks for the help."

Leaving Greg's office, Matt made a quick stop by his squadron to check in. Most of the teams were out training or on active operations, so he didn't bother lingering. Matt grabbed his bag, along with some extra gear, and left the headquarters. It was time to shake out some more pieces to this puzzle.

Matt dropped the stack of mail on the kitchen counter before walking over and setting his bag on the table. Sifting through the advertisements and credit-card applications for anything useful, he discarded months' worth of mail into the trash can. Although the apartment was barely lived-in, Matt figured he had better take the time to reset everything before diving back into work. Starting with the pile of laundry he'd been neglecting since returning from the Philippines.

Folding a stack of shirts, he couldn't help but wonder if he was getting a glimpse of the rest of his life—returning from an assignment to a near-empty apartment that was technically his but somehow seemed foreign. Matt had never minded being alone or bouncing around the country to scoop up operational assignments, but the downside of his career path was that he never stayed anywhere long enough to build lasting relationships. With the pace and type of operations he would be kept on in the unit, there would be even less chance now. Unit members who were married tended to have met their spouses long before selection, and even then, more than a fair share of these marriages ended in one way or another. For the time being, he would gladly continue this life, but he wondered if he would look back one day and wish he had chosen differently.

Laundry either repacked or put away, floors swept, and freshly delivered curry in hand, Matt unloaded his bag onto the kitchen table. He picked up Chen's work computer and traced his finger along the puncture marks before placing the device face down and grabbing a screwdriver. Removing the dozen screws, he separated the case to expose the components inside. The knife had punctured the motherboard in several places and cracked the processor, so there was no chance the device would run again, but Matt didn't really care about that.

He just needed the hard drive to be intact. Removing another small piece of plastic frame, he realized he wasn't so lucky. The knife had found the drive and pierced through the thin metal case. Inside, Matt could hear pieces of the disk rattling around. Reassembling the damaged computer, he put it back into his bag. It wasn't going to be of any use to him.

Turning his attention to the home computer, Matt repeated the process of removing the outer case and exposing the components inside. Similar holes marked the motherboard on this device as well, but when he took out the hard drive, it looked intact. Removing the connectors from the small drive, he slid the broken laptop to the side and placed his own computer in front of him. While it was booting up, he removed a small device from his bag, connecting one end to the hard drive and the other to the USB port on his computer. He opened his exploitation software, selected the cloning program, and hit Run.

Matt sat back in his chair, finishing off the container of chicken vindaloo and watching the progress bar creep toward completion. One percent. Matt switched his attention to his phone and read through his news feed. Two percent. *This is going to take a while*, he thought. Fortunately, he didn't actually have to stare at it for the program to work. Leaving the system to run its course, he went to sleep.

Waking with the sun in his eyes, Matt started coffee and went to check on the progress of the program. The transfer registered as complete, and the automatic error-detection process had also finished without uncovering any problems. Matt unplugged the hard drive, reassembled the second broken machine, and put it back in his bag. With a virtual image of the device now loaded into his computer, he could exploit its contents without fear of corrupting it.

Dr. Chen's work email account loaded automatically when Matt opened the internet browser. Looking through the inbox and sent items, Matt found nothing from the past few weeks that would suggest the professor was in any sort of trouble, beyond a few students who were unhappy with their grades on a recent exam. A scroll through the browser's history and the messenger application returned similar results. There was nothing that indicated Chen had felt he was in any sort of danger, and Matt decided to set that line of inquiry aside.

Turning to the reason he had flown out to see the professor in the first place, he opened a search tool and ran a query for any mention of neodymium. Matt looked at the long list of results and sighed, knowing how long it would take him to work through them all. But not before he had a shower.

Clean and caffeinated, Matt waded into the files. Skimming the titles and abstracts of each one, he became more and more convinced that Dr. Chen had assembled the entire body of human knowledge on neodymium on his computer—and that most of it was both meaningless to a non-scientist and useless to his current needs. After an hour of striking out, Matt was less than halfway through the list. Feeling his frustration rising, he was about to stop for a break when something caught his attention. He scrolled back up and centered the picture on his screen, staring at it intently. The rendered image, which took up half a page, showed a large black cube centered around a larger circuit board with metal fins protruding from its top. Matt thought back to the system he had found in the Philippines and tried to imagine what it would look like had it not melted. Looking at the caption underneath the image, Matt read:

Prototype design 6.8 for neodymium composite quantum core.

Could this be it? he asked himself. Returning to the top of the document, he began reading more closely. After the third page, he gave up pretending to understand what Dr. Chen was saying through the highly technical language. Matt wasn't a computer architect, and wasn't about to become one in an afternoon. As he continued reading, though, it became clear that this document described the design for an advanced computer system. It also became apparent that if this was, in fact, describing the melted device sitting on his kitchen table, then Matt would need to find an expert to help him understand what this was. Matt closed his laptop and repacked his bag, leaving out Dr. Chen's computers. No need to carry those around anymore since one was dead and the other lived in a virtual instance on his system. Switching off the lights, Matt headed out of his apartment toward the garage.

Chapter 6

"Excuse me, do you know if Dr. Nascent is around?" Matt asked, poking his head into an open office.

"Um . . . I saw him earlier today," a young woman said. "But I'm not sure where he's gone off to now. He gets pulled into meetings across town all the time, though, so it wouldn't surprise me if that's where he was. If so, he's normally gone for three or four hours."

"Ah, OK. Thanks. Do you have a sticky note I can use to leave him a message?"

"Sure," she said, handing him a small block of notes.

Matt took one and returned the block. "Thanks for your help," he said as he turned to leave. Outside of Dr. Nascent's office, he wrote a quick note along with his phone number and stuck it to the door. Checking his watch, he figured that it would be worth it to stick around the building and wait for Dr. Nascent, and that he might as well grab coffee from the shop on the ground floor and see what else he could find in Chen's files.

In the café, Matt ordered black coffee from the bar and looked for the best place to sit. His eyes landed on a familiar face. Since he had some time to kill, he walked over.

"Where's your friend? I figured I might try to run into him

again," Matt said with a smile.

"Oh, hi," Drew replied. "He's probably off assaulting some unsuspecting person somewhere. That does seem to be his thing."

"If you don't mind, can you tell his latest victim that a few of us have formed a survivors group that meets at the church down the road?"

"Another one? There are chapters popping up everywhere," Drew laughed.

"Do you mind if I sit?"

"Sure, go ahead," she said, motioning to the seat across from her. "I was actually just texting him. Again. He ran off a couple days ago. He never came home, and I can't reach his phone either."

"Is that unusual for him?" Matt asked, setting his backpack next to the wall and sitting down.

"It is. I've known his since we were freshmen, and this hasn't ever happened before. I'm not normally one to jump to conclusions, but he's been acting strangely for the last few weeks. I'm starting to get a little worried."

"Do you think he's breaking up with you?"

Drew looked startled by the question, and shook her head.

"Oh, God no. We aren't together like that. Ish is my best friend and roommate, but I've known him since freshman year. I've seen too much to know that would never work out." She laughed.

"Ah, bad assumption on my part then, sorry. You mentioned he was acting strangely. How so?"

"I don't know. It's hard to describe. He's been a little more aloof than usual. He didn't want to tell me about the late-night dates he's had a couple of times, sticking around the office longer, stuff like that. Nothing that is in and of itself a red flag, but in the aggregate, it seems off. And ever since I saw him get into some random car with a guy that looked way more like a chauffeur than an uber driver the other night, something just really doesn't feel right. The fact that he now doesn't return my calls is only causing me to spiral further and further down the rabbit hole."

"What do you mean, 'random car'?" Matt asked.

Before she could answer, Drew's phone rang. "Oh, well, speak of the devil," she said, picking it up. "Ish, where the hell are you? I've been worried sick." There was slightly more harshness in her tone than she had meant.

"Yeah, sorry to ghost you like that," Ish said. "It's been a rough couple of days. My grandfather passed away on Friday, and I came back home to be with my family. I've been kind of out of it. I can't believe he's gone." His voice trailed off.

"Oh my gosh, Ish, I'm so sorry. What can I do?" Drew said.

"No, it's OK. I'm a jerk. I should have called you. There's not really anything you can do. The funeral service is tomorrow, and I'm going to take a couple more days down here before coming back to DC. It just . . . sucks."

"OK, well if there is anything I can do, please let me know. I'm sorry."

"Thanks. I'll check in with you later."

"Do that. Or I'll hunt you down," Drew said.

Ish hung up, and Drew put the phone back down on the table, and then stared at it. Thumbing the lip of her coffee cup, she looked up at Matt. "Well, I guess I've solved that mystery. He said his grandfather just died so he went home. I'm both relieved and upset at the same time. I don't know. It's weird."

"It would be worse if you didn't care at all. I'm sure it means a lot to him," Matt said, trying to reassure her.

"Yeah. What brings you back down here?"

"I have something I wanted to run by Dr. Nascent again, but it seems like he's out at a meeting and won't be back for a while. I figured I'd grab coffee and wait for him here."

"Well, you're going to need more coffee. Dr. Nascent and my boss are in a meeting. But it's in New York. For the whole week."

"Oh," Matt replied. "Well, that sucks. I suppose I'll just have to come back next week then."

"What did you want to ask him?"

"I came across a paper on some system and I was hoping he might be able to help me decipher it. Computer engineering isn't exactly my strong suit."

"Huh. Well, I'm nowhere near as good as Dr. Nascent, but I could take a look at it if you'd like." Drew offered.

Matt looked at the young woman sitting across from him. Without any of the additional context, there was no way that having her look at the unclassified academic paper would compromise anything sensitive, so he decided there was no harm in showing her what he had found.

"Sure. I'm Matt, by the way."

"Drew. Nice to meet you. So, what do you have?"

Matt took his laptop out of his bag and set it on the table. Clicking open the document, he turned the computer around to face Drew, who pulled it closer to her, adjusted the angle of the screen, and began reading. Matt sat quietly drinking his coffee and watched as Drew read through the file. After about ten minutes, Drew sat up.

"Did someone actually build this?" she asked.

"What is it?" Matt asked, redirecting the question.

"This is a design for a quantum computer," she replied, "but it's totally different than any of the stuff I've seen before."

"What do you mean? What's a quantum computer?"

"You're obviously familiar with a traditional computer," Drew said, pointing to the laptop. "When we first started experimenting with these a hundred years ago, scientists and mathematicians were super excited about the possibilities. They built computers that took up entire rooms, and even though the initial designs were rudimentary, they were still way faster at performing calculations than a human. They could perform in moments what would take a human days to work out by hand. The world changed forever as people figured out how to unleash the power of these new machines. Right now, we're sitting in the exact same place with quantum computers. The idea is to use the properties of quantum physics to our advantage.

"You see, in a traditional computer, each bit of data can either be a one or a zero, which ultimately becomes our limiting factor. Quantum computers, however, use qubits that can be multiple things at once. I'm not a physicist, so don't ask me to explain it any more than that. The point is, now calculations that would take the most advanced supercomputers years to complete could be solved instantly."

"So it's a really fast computer," Matt said.

"In the same way that a supercomputer is a really fast abacus, yes."

"You said this one is different. Why do you think that?"

"Look, I'm totally out of my depth here. I don't really know anything about these sorts of systems. But what I have seen is that most of them are pretty massive. Since the whole field is still in its infancy, they take up huge amounts of space in labs and require all sorts of extra systems for environmental controls to keep everything running. But this design is really no bigger than some traditional servers you would find in any IT department. I don't want to say there's no way this thing would work, but it just doesn't make any sense to me. Why did you want to get Dr. Nascent to look at this? Is this actually real? Did someone build it?"

"What would you do with a system like this?" Matt asked, redirecting again.

"Well, since I'm in AI development, that's what I would do. I would run an AI on this thing that would outperform any AI on the planet because it could work through datasets so fast. The new types of problems it could learn to solve would be amazing. So, since you're here and you keep avoiding my question, I'm going to go ahead and say that yes, someone has built it. And you're here at DARPA, so I'm guessing that you're in the military. Otherwise, you would have gone to MIT or Cal Tech for answers. And the fact that you're coming to us and not the other way around, whoever built it is probably not American. Plus, you're giving me your best poker face. How am I doing?"

Matt tried to figure out what expression was on his face so that he could practice not making it in the future. "Well, you're not completely wrong, but I'm afraid that's the best I can give you," he admitted after a long pause.

"That's fine. You can keep your secrets. Hopefully I was at least able to get you a little farther down your path. Whatever that might be. I've got to run back up to the office now. It was nice to meet you, Matt the Mysterious," Drew said. Smiling, she got up from her seat.

"Very much so, thanks. Next time coffee is on me," Matt said.

As he watched her walk out the door, Matt felt the phone in his pocket vibrate with an incoming message. Looking at the screen, Matt couldn't help but smile at the impeccable timing. Just the man he needed to go see.

-

Climbing the stairs up to the front porch, Matt checked his phone once more out of habit and rang the bell.

"Matt, how big of a jackass are you?" a voice came through the smart doorbell. "You know full well that a guy with a shattered hip isn't in any shape to get off his recliner to answer the door. Get your ass in here, and grab me a drink from the fridge while you're at it."

Opening the door and slipping off his shoes, Matt called out, "I see the near-death experience has done nothing for your personality, Dean."

"Yeah, yeah. Less talk, more drink. Shannon left at seven thirty, and I am running dangerously low on supplies over here."

"Well, let's just see if we can fix that, then, huh?" Matt said, holding out both a beer and a Gatorade.

Dean picked the Gatorade and twisted off the cap. "Exactly what I need to get my electrolytes up for a run later."

"For some reason, there is the slightest hint of doubt within me that you actually might be serious."

"I'm going nuts, man. I need to get out of the house. Something. There's only so many times I can rewatch *Point Break*."

"Not sure I can help you with the getting out of the house, but I do have something I could use your help with. Give you something to mull over, and fill a few minutes of boredom" Matt pulled his laptop out of his bag.

"Now we're talking. What did you bring me?"

"I'm still trying to chase down that device from the Philippines. After some poking around, I got my hands on a design for something that might be what we found there." Matt pulled up the file and passed the computer to Dean. "Best guess right now is that it's some new computer system built around a quantum processor, which makes it way more powerful than anything anybody else is running right now. But I still don't know what it does, or what they were doing with it. Just that it was a quantum computer, the people who installed it knew that it was going to get really hot, and that when I got there it had catastrophically melted down. I'm kind of stuck here, though, and I'm not sure where to go."

Dean skimmed through the file and then leaned back in his chair to think. Finally, he turned to Matt and spoke. "We know more than that. We know that from the time it was switched on to the time it failed was about seven days. Maybe a little less, since it was cool enough for you to mess with when you found it. Based on what this design says, we also know that it draws a ridiculous amount of power. Not to mention the extra cost associated with cooling the rest of the server room.

"What if we search for that anomaly? Instances of major telecom facilities that experienced significant power spikes lasting around a week. We might first check to see if this correlates to the events that sent us down there in the first place."

"Is that something that Conner's analysts would be able to find for us? Do they have access to that sort of telemetry?" Matt asked.

"Won't know unless we ask him."

Dean picked up his work phone off the end table, put it into secure mode, and pulled up the number to the unit's intelligence director. After a quick exchange, he hung up.

"He says he needs a couple hours, but he should be able to get us something."

"Perfect. Just enough time to watch Johnny Utah infiltrate that gang of adrenaline-junkie thieves," Matt said, smiling at Dean.

"I changed my mind. Hand me that beer. And the remote."

Dean's phone rang just as Patrick Swayze's character ran back out to catch one last wave.

"You sure? No, yeah. Send whatever you've got to Matt and I, and we'll take a look," Dean said. "And thanks."

"So?"

"Four of the five events had that anomaly, and he couldn't rule out it being there in the fifth."

"Holy shit."

"Yeah, man. You just connected them all together. Lockheed, Nigeria, Iraq, and now the Philippines. Every time they seem to put in a cheat code to read minds, this device is there. I'd be willing to bet that there was one behind the knocking out of our source network as well. We just don't have the data on that. I think we're looking at some sort of device that can spy on our communications systems. Even though they're heavily encrypted. Which is nuts, because the AES-256 algorithm would take millions of years for any other computer to break."

"But if a quantum processor can do what these papers seem to think they can do, it would only take a second to decrypt," Matt said. "They could have total access to every single piece of information streaming through that telecom hub."

"You need to go tell the colonel."

Chapter 7

Frank walked into the bare concrete building and shook his head. After the meeting he had just finished at the First Military District headquarters, he should have expected the less-than-warm reception to continue. He couldn't blame the Vietnamese staff officers, though. Nobody likes being told that outsiders are going to come into their territory to work, especially when those outsiders are foreigners. Lieutenant Nguyen had handled himself well despite the massive difference in rank between him and the district's chief of staff. The entire joint coordination session was mostly a formality, though, as orders had come straight from Hanoi, and everyone in that room had known it. Still, Frank thought, the offer of support from the chief of staff at the end had been genuine. As long as they didn't impose too much, he guessed that the command would come through with anything his team needed.

Their first need had been a base of operations. Despite the spartan accommodations, this small compound was actually well suited for their needs. Far enough off of the main road to go unnoticed, the seven buildings provided adequate space for both the ODA and the Ranger platoon. The town of Bac Kan was a short drive away for most of their logistics needs, and the city of Thai Nguyen was ninety minutes down the road—just far enough from the military-district headquarters there to be left alone.

Frank walked outside and made his way back to the team's truck. "All right, fellas," he said as the four other Green Berets moved in closer, "the LT's going to be setting up his platoon in those first three buildings at the south end of the compound. That gives us the three on the northwest corner to play with, leaving the large garage in the middle as a workspace for whoever needs it. Plenty of room for everyone."

Seeing nods from everyone, Frank continued. "Eli, any of these buildings strike your fancy as being better to get comms run into?"

"No, sir. They're all about the same. If I had my preference, though, I'd pick the one on the right there. Shorter cable run for my antennas."

"Works for me. Tim, I'll leave it up to you to draft up the security plan. Grab whoever you need when it's time to install the cameras. There's no reason to expect any trouble, but we might as well get everything set up just the same. Same with you, Doc. Figure out where you're going to want to hand out Motrin. I got a note from Rizzo that they had picked up everything on their shopping list and were headed this way. They should get in later tonight. Chief, let's start getting our systems up and running. Then we should bring the LT in and come up with our plan."

The huddle complete, each man went about his task. Frank and CW2 Mike Smith, the ODA's warrant officer and assistant commander, shouldered their rucks and picked up two of the black transit cases from the back of a gray Toyota Hilux, carrying them into their new command post. Over the course of the afternoon, the four men turned the corner of an empty cinder-block compound into a workable staging base.

A little after ten o'clock, four additional vehicles drove into the compound with Rizzo and the rest of the team. Frank went out to greet them.

"Damn, Rizzo," Frank said, looking into the back of each vehicle. "Was there anything you didn't bring with you?"

The master sergeant grinned as he pulled his lanky frame from behind the wheel of a well-worn Mazda hatchback. "Sir, it's far better to be prepared for these sorts of things. Plus, look who I found at the airport."

Frank watched as the passenger door opened and saw a kid, probably just barely old enough to drink, get out.

"Captain Gonzales, I would like to introduce you to Specialist Brian Ortiz. He's the SIGINT guy the Group sent us to help track down whatever ghosts are running around here. In addition to being great at tactical signals intelligence, he also speaks fluent Swahili . . . which would be great if we were within a thousand miles of East Africa."

"Well, he put up with you for the entire trip up here, so he must be doing all right. Great to meet you, Ortiz."

The rest of the team slowly peeled themselves out of the assorted vehicles and unpacked. By midnight, the compound had fallen silent.

-

Hearing commotion in the room, Frank slipped out of his sleeping bag and sat up on the cot. He had always preferred sleeping in the command post, hating the thought of not being available if something were to pop up. In this case, the morning's action was just Chief Smith making coffee. Still,

Frank thought, not an event to be missed. He put on a pair of khaki pants, a blue polo shirt, and a faded Red Sox cap and walked across the room.

"Good morning, Chief," he said, filling his travel mug from the carafe. "How are we doing?"

"I think we're on the right side of the equation, at least for the time being. Looks like Rizzo got just about everything we requested in that logistics package, which is a small miracle. We should spend most of the day getting us and the LT up to speed on the situation. It's almost 1500 back home, so they've had all day to fill our inboxes with information of varying utility. Hopefully the S2 has some start points for the kid to work off of. He's young, but the sergeant major swears he's one of the best SIGINTers that's come through the SOT-A in a while."

"Yeah, that works for me," Frank said. The cheap plastic chair buckled slightly as he sat down. After bracing himself for a collapse that didn't come, he opened the lid of his laptop and booted up the system. As he read through the reports in his inbox, the rest of the team slowly trickled in.

"What's the word, sir?" Tim asked, shaking a water bottle to mix in the pre-workout the large man seemed to live off of.

Frank looked up at Tim. "There haven't been any more reports of unusual activity coming in from the intel folks. I think we're going to spend today doing some area familiarization with the Rangers. It's going to take a while for us to get a lay of the land, and the better we know this place, the easier of a time we'll have once something does pop up. How are we looking on initial set up tasks? Is there still anything outstanding that we need to take care of?

"Sir, I'd like to throw up a couple force-protection sensors if we have time," Eli said. "The cameras are good, but it would be better if we could augment them. I don't think that would take me more than a couple of hours, though."

"Probably a good idea," Frank replied. "We can snag you once you're done. Let's go see what Lieutenant Nguyen has his boys up to this morning, shall we?"

Closing his laptop, Frank slid his pistol into the concealed holster behind his hip and finished the rest of his coffee. After the rest of the team had finished their morning routines, they walked together to the other side of the compound.

"LT, how are we doing this morning?" Frank asked.

"Very good, Captain. We are still waiting on our gear to arrive, but it will do us no good to stand around until it gets here."

"Couldn't agree more. We thought the best thing to do would be some area familiarization with your platoon to get a feel for this place. It would be great if anyone from your platoon who is from the area could ride along with us. What we're interested in is understanding the road networks, where the key terrain features are in the area, what the most likely places for foreigners to spend time would be, things like that."

"Yes, this is prudent. I do have two soldiers from this area who can accompany you. I will have them identify themselves to Sergeant Mac. Have you received any new updates on the trespassers?"

"No, nothing yet. That might be a good thing, though. That will let us get up and running in the area and check out some of the old reporting. All of that prep work will improve our odds of success if another incursion is detected. If nothing pops up, though, we will have gotten a nice holiday of sightseeing this part of the country."

"Let us hope you are correct, Captain, and this is nothing serious."

For the next three days, the Green Berets and Rangers drove the main roads, secondary streets, and alleys around the province. Stopping at cafés, restaurants, and hotels, they cataloged traffic flow, activity levels, security, and any other useful information to help the group understand how people moved throughout the area.

Once they had a good sense for getting around the region, the team turned their attention to the reported movements of the previous Chinese incursion, starting from the north and tracing each one as it moved across the province. Although no clear actions and intentions came out of this exercise, Frank and the team found a couple likely points of convergence for movement patterns that could be useful if they detected another cross-border movement.

As the last rays of light dipped below the horizon, Frank walked into the CP and dropped his bag. "Well, Dave," he said, sitting next to the ODA's intel specialist, "what did we learn today?"

"Sir, welcome back," Dave asked. "Did you successfully drink a cup of coffee from every café in northern Vietnam?"

"I feel like I'm pretty damned close. Maybe another day or two and we'll have a clean sweep."

"Well, I don't have the news you're hoping for. No new activity reported. I've spent most of my days trying to refine the pattern of life from the last couple of events. Because we didn't have anyone pulling real-time data when they were here, there are a lot of holes in what we know. I think it might be worthwhile to pursue Chief's theory that there's something special about that restaurant on the western edge of Bac Kan, though. Even if it's nothing more than word's gotten out about their pho being extra delicious, it still gives us a known point to work from. For now, we're really just in a waiting game to see if we get lucky and pick up when another team comes over."

"Such is the life of the hunter sometimes."

Rizzo walked up to the desk. "Given how well the past couple of days have gone, I'd recommend taking a day off and working on some surveillance techniques with the team," he said. "Everyone is pretty burned out from spending all day on the road, and it'll come in handy to refresh everyone in case we find an opportunity to get up close and personal."

"Good idea," Frank said. "I'll let the LT know when I go over there in a bit. I don't think he'll be upset for the change of pace. You all ready to eat? I'm going to make sure there's nothing hot in my inbox and then I'll be ready to dig into whatever Eli snagged on the way back here."

Frank read through the few emails that were waiting for him, and responded to the two information requests from his company commander. The rest of his administrative tasks could wait until after dinner and a call home to Kathy. Shutting down his computer, he walked across the interior of the compound to the central building. Sergeant Tran had set up enough tables and chairs to accommodate the entire group. As Frank approached the open bay, he could hear laughter spilling out into the night.

"Boys, how are we living?" he asked, walking up to a large group sitting around a table.

"Sir, pull up a chair," Rizzo said. "Tim was just regaling us with tales of an ill-spent youth."

Frank pulled up a chair and sat down. "Oh, please don't stop on my account. Where were we, Tim?"

"I was talking about how crazy the life of a college football player was."

"You played tight end for Arkansas, right?" Frank asked.

"Razorbacks all the way, sir," Tim confirmed.

"Tim wasn't talking about his exploits on the field, though, if you know what I mean," Rizzo prodded.

"To finish that story," Tim continued, "I have no idea how we didn't get arrested. Half of us were so drunk they ended up passing out in the front lawn. When the cops showed up, I was pretty sure my life was over. We had beaten Alabama earlier that day, though, so the two officers weren't about to arrest the QB and running back. That's just how we rolled, though. We'd crush ourselves all week during practice, give everything we had on Saturday afternoons, and then put that same intensity into partying Saturday night. We'd wake up Sunday and do it all over again. Man, that was a great time." Tim said.

"You didn't want to continue those shenanigans and play at the pro level?" Eli asked.

"I did. I was good enough to play college ball, but not enough to last in the NFL. I got cut from the Panthers after one season."

"And now you get to hang out with us," Rizzo said.

"Well, yeah. Getting cut was rough. Football was my life, and without that thing I was lost. I wasn't sure what to do. I'd kept up with one of my high school teammates who had gone into the Army after we graduated, so I reached out and asked him about his experience. He said he enjoyed what he did, but told me to look into the 18X program. Walked into the recruiter's office the next day."

"My biggest takeaway from this story is that Eli and Mac

need to get college-kid drunk and pass out in the courtyard so that Tim here can feel at home," Rizzo laughed.

"Hard pass," Eli said. "My liver still hasn't forgiven me for what I did to it after basic training."

"Boots, booze, and bad decisions—name a better trio," Mac said.

-

Frank startled awake on his cot to the chime of an incoming message. He rolled over and picked up his phone. Swiping past the lock-screen picture of Kyra from her first ski trip, he opened his messages. *Check your email.* Even if they forgot that ten a.m. back on the west coast was one a.m. in Vietnam, no one at group would bother sending both an email and a text unless it was necessary. Frank stepped into his running shoes and pulled a hoodie on while he shuffled over to the desk. Hitting the power button on his laptop, he alternated between bringing his computer online and getting the coffee brewing. Half asleep, he wasn't sure which was more important. The computer won, so he sat down and opened the email client while the coffeepot continued gurgling in the background. Sitting at the top of his inbox was a note from the SOCPAC intel team in Hawaii.

CPT Gonzales,

We've gotten new reports that another possible Chinese reconnaissance team crossed the border a few hours ago north of Dong Dang. Best we can tell from where they crossed, they did so on foot, but it is likely that they either have a car staged for them or someone will be picking them up. Our current assessment is that there are three individuals.

There is additional technical reporting that your intel sergeant can use waiting for him on his system. That data is going to get stale quickly, however, and we're not sure if or when we will get another glimpse of them.

Will keep you updated on anything else we find from back here.

v/r

LCDR Tom Burke

SOCPAC J2 Deputy

Frank walked past the coffeepot and out of the office. It would have to wait a few more minutes while he woke up the rest of the team. Once outside, he flicked on his headlamp and jogged through the warm midnight air. Although he was running on low sleep, he felt more alive than he had in a long time. This was why he'd joined, he thought, to help smaller countries against real threats, and not just taking them to a range and talking about what might happen over dinner. A smile spread across his face as he opened the door to where the rest of the team was sleeping.

"Rizzo, Chief," Frank said as he nudged their cots, "Wake up. We've got a hit. Get the boys up and going. I'm going to go find the LT. I'll meet you back in the CP."

The two men looked at Frank for a moment while his words pierced the half-asleep fog.

"Got it, sir," Rizzo finally said. "It's about time we did something useful around here."

With proof that at least one of them was awake enough to hear what he had just said, Frank turned and walked out of the room. Behind him, he heard the team sergeant's voice echo off the cinder-block walls. A minute later, he stood outside one of the Ranger platoon's buildings and knocked on the door. Like

Frank, Lieutenant Nguyen slept in his office rather than in the building they had set up as a barracks. After a second round of knocking, he could hear feet shuffling across the floor, so he stood back from the door, waiting for it to open.

"Oh, good night, Captain," Lieutenant Nguyen said. "What can I do for you at this hour?"

"LT, I just got word that another possible recon team crossed the border a few hours ago. I'm getting my team up and running to look through the initial reporting and figuring out a plan to find these guys. I think it's going to take us a few hours to work through everything before we're ready to move, so there's no need to kick your platoon out of bed yet. But if you wanted to run anything by your command to see if they have seen anything or if there is anything else you needed to prepare, I wanted to make sure you had the option."

"Thank you, Captain. As you said. I will let my soldiers sleep a little longer, but will make some calls to see what I can find out. I will join you once I am ready, if that is suitable to you."

"Thanks, LT. Hell of a way to start the morning, no?" Frank said. From the other side of the compound, it looked like the CP's light slowly flashed on and off as the twelve other members of the ODA came through the door, momentarily spilling the light as they entered. Frank walked back over to their side of the compound. Passing through the door, Mac handed him his coffee cup.

"These cretins were about to leave you high and dry, sir," Mac said. "But don't you worry. I've got you. Just remember this the next time you need to pick someone for some bullshit tasking. Mac's got your back. It rhymes, so it must be true."

"Sir," Chris Salvatore chimed in, "the only bullshit you need to watch out for is currently streaming out of Mac's mouth.

I am prepared to collect sworn statements from the entire detachment and the new specialist here detailing a heinous plot by one Staff Sergeant Brian Mackinzie to deprive you of mission-critical caffeine."

"I see we're starting early today," Frank said, eyeing his two medics, "Well, we have bigger things at the moment that demand our attention, but should such a conspiracy actually exist within these walls, then those conspirators are now on notice. I have eyes everywhere, gentlemen."

Frank moved over to the corner of the room where several maps and a whiteboard hung on the wall. "SOCPAC J2 has another possible Chinese reconnaissance team of three potentially crossing the border north of Dong Dang. There's nothing else around there but jungle, so why they wouldn't just come across through the border checkpoint raises suspicion. Although they pretty much had to make that crossing on foot, chances are good that they either staged a car or someone picked them up."

Looking at the young SIGINT specialist, Frank continued, "Ortiz, there should be additional technical information waiting for you to pull down that should give us a little more information on how to find these guys. If you want to work on that, the rest of us will start getting everything prepped."

"Sir, I'll help Ortiz since this is his first time out here." Frank turned to look as SFC Dave Wolters, the team's intelligence sergeant, began speaking. "If they send him what they usually do, there are a couple of things that will make him much faster and fill in a few more pieces."

"Thanks, Dave," Frank replied. He watched the two men walk across to the far side of the CP, and then turned back to the rest of the group. "We can't really do any specific planning until they figure out where we're going, but there's still a lot of work we can do. Vehicle maintenance, communications checks, loadouts, all of the normal pre-mission activities. The sooner we knock those out for us, the sooner we can lend a hand to the Rangers. Does anyone have any questions or anything to add?"

Frank looked around at the team, giving them time to speak up. "All right, then let's get to work. Chief, let's start fleshing out our general scheme of maneuver."

"Where did those dry-erase markers run off to?" Mike asked, opening up the box of office supplies. "Ah, here we go."

Frank and Mike talked through a few different scenarios based on what Ortiz and Dave had pulled from the intel reports while the rest of the team filtered in and out between the CP and the vehicles outside. Finally, Dave returned with Ortiz in tow to tell Frank what they had found.

"Sir, I think we've got two likely start points, and another few if those don't pan out," Dave said, pointing to one of the pins on the wall map. "My first recommendation is the Hotel del Luna in Lang Son. They've based out of there before, and it would make sense that they would want to reset after their infil before continuing on with whatever they're doing. There are a couple other hotels in the immediate vicinity, too, that would meet that requirement."

"Makes sense. What's your second guess?" Frank asked.

"The same thing but in the other direction. If they don't go to Lang Son, they often end up in Cao Bang at La Maison Hotel."

"We've got enough people and vehicles to cover both options adequately," Mike said. "I'd split the team and see what we can find. Dave, you're spun up on the extra kit that Ortiz brought, yeah? We could put one of you with each element to try and get a ping off of one of their devices."

"My thoughts exactly, Chief," Dave said.

"Well, we've got to start somewhere," Frank said. "Let's round up the team and grab the LT. Time to go fishing."

Dave gave the same intelligence assessment again once the team had reassembled. After he finished, Frank took over. "So Chief and his team are going to head for Lang Son, and I'll take mine to Cao Bang with Lieutenant Nguyen. Our objective for this first shot is to pick up the trail. Once we have that, we'll transition to tracking their movement and trying to figure out what they're up to. LT, let's hold the rest of your platoon, teams three and four, here so we aren't burning everything we have right out of the gate and can react to any opportunities that pop up."

"Very good, Captain," Lieutenant Nguyen said. "They will remain ready. We are also inquiring through our networks to identify the group of three Chinese travelers. They have instructions to alert me should anything be discovered."

"All right, if they are moving to a hotel as a bed-down location like Mike seems to think, we've got a brief window to find them before they start doing whatever they're doing," Frank added to close out the huddle.

Over the next thirty minutes, both teams finished up the last of their preparations, ran through their standard pre-mission briefing, and climbed into the vehicles.

Sitting in the passenger seat of an early-2000s gray Mazda hatchback, Frank positioned the GPS on the dashboard and picked up the small handheld radio from the cup holder. "All right, team one, let's head out. We'll call out the turns as we approach them. Call in once your vehicle is ready to move."

Switching over to his cell phone, he opened his messaging app.

Good luck Mike. Let me know if you run into anything.

Loser buys dinner for the team. Stay safe, Mike returned.

With everyone on his team ready, Frank nodded to Tim, who put the car into gear and rolled out of the compound and onto the main road.

Chapter 8

After three hours on the road, Frank's team rolled into Cao Bang. Since Ortiz and the LT were in his vehicle, they drove all the way up to the side of the hotel. The soldiers in the remaining three vehicles parked several blocks away, just off the main roads, and watched.

"All right, Ortiz," Frank said, "find me some Chinese spies."

"I'm on it, sir," Ortiz replied. He reached into his backpack, powered on his equipment, and set the laptop on his knees. "I have a couple of hints from the guys at SOCPAC, but this is definitely the hard part. Once we know what we're looking for it'll be much easier."

"You've got this," Frank reassured him. "LT, there should be a decent café inside the hotel lobby. Would be a great place to keep an eye on the front lobby."

"Yes, that will be good. I have my mobile if you must contact me," Lieutenant Nguyen replied, opening up the Mazda's rear door and stepping onto the sidewalk.

Frank continued to monitor the movement of the team in and around Cao Bang and periodically checked in with Mike. In between, he stared out the windshield of the car, watching people fill the streets.

"How are we looking, Ortiz?" Frank asked, breaking the

silence.

"Sir, I have everything dialed in. So far, though, I don't see anything. I think if we don't get a hit in the next half hour or so, we should relocate to a different part of the building. If nothing there, then we start expanding our search."

"Works for me," Frank said.

Thirty minutes later, Frank had Tim move the car to the opposite corner of the building. Thirty minutes after that, he called Lieutenant Nguyen back. Once the LT was back in the car, Frank opened the map application on his phone and discussed the next move with his Vietnamese counterpart.

"All right, Tim, take us here," Frank said as he loaded the directions into the GPS. "Ortiz, keep monitoring, and let me know if you find anything." While Tim pulled out into traffic, Frank relayed their repositioning to the rest of the team.

As soon as they had settled into their next position, Frank's phone vibrated.

Bingo. Dave picked up two of the three and has a solid lock on them. Right where he said they would be. We are going to set up for a follow. Sergeant Tran is getting another team out here to support. Looks like you owe us dinner. I'm thinking seafood.

Frank relayed the message to the rest of his team over the radio and had them get ready to move out. He turned to the back seat.

"LT, do you think you can coordinate a place for two teams to forward-stage out of near Lang Son? We don't need to move everything yet, but making that drive routinely is going to wear us out too quickly."

"Yes, Captain. I will place a call to someone who I think will be able to help us."

Three more hours in the passenger seat meant that Frank

had to unfold himself to get out once they finally stopped. Lieutenant Nguyen had managed to get the team a large house on the southern end of Lang Son to use as a temporary staging point, and as Frank surveyed the surrounding area, he couldn't help but wonder how much a place like this would cost. Frank and the rest of his team went inside the house and made themselves comfortable in the living room. Rizzo and the third team were set to arrive from Bac Kan in the next twenty minutes to pick up Ortiz and go out to replace Mike on watch, so Frank would have about five hours to recover from the day and talk through the plan with Mike before it was his team's watch. Until Mike got there, though, there wasn't much for Frank to do, so he found one of the bedrooms, stretched out on top of the bed, and fell asleep.

Lifting the bill of his hat, Frank opened an eye to see who had just smacked his shoe.

"Good morning, princess," Mike said.

"Hey, Chief. I see you finally found the place." Frank swung his legs off the side of the bed.

"Eh, I got here twenty or thirty minutes ago. Figured I'd let you sleep a little longer while we got situated. Fancy place the LT found."

"Definitely better than some of the places we've ended up, that's for sure. Let me take a piss and then you can fill me in on your find."

Frank walked back downstairs and found the dining room transformed into a temporary CP. Rizzo had dropped off some supplies and Tim and Eli had gotten to work setting up their light comms package and analog planning tools. He walked up to Mike, who was talking with Lieutenant Nguyen next to the wall map.

"Dave was right on the money. We got into town and set up on the north side of the hotel, but we were a little far. After about twenty minutes, we re-positioned around to the west. Took Dave all of three minutes to find the first one and another four to tag the second. Sergeant Tran sent one of his guys in to take a look inside the building, and the rest of the team posted up so we had eyes on all of the major egress points. Transitioning with Rizzo was pretty much the same. They kicked out a couple guys on foot so we could offset the vehicle exchanges a little bit, but didn't have any movement. I think we're in a pretty good spot."

"And now we wait."

"Three Chinese males exiting the front door." The radio sprang to life as Gary, the weapons sergeant, began reporting the movement. "Looks like they're heading towards the parking lot."

"Apparently we do not have to wait very long," Lieutenant Nguyen replied.

"Let's set up to follow in case that's them." Rizzo's voice came in calm and clear over the net as he began directing his team. "Gary, you've got the eye and are prepped to cover south. Mac, your vehicle is already in position to cover if they head north. Rizzo, you take second position for either. I'll keep posted here with Dave to make sure those are our guys before we break and follow. Remember, we don't know what you don't tell us, so communicate, communicate, communicate. Let's do this."

"Vehicle on the move. Blue four-door Toyota. License plate three-zero-Y-six-six-five. Turning north. I have the eye."

Frank pulled up Google Maps for the city and tried to follow along.

"Right turn. Second right. Quick left. Looks like they're going south on the highway. Rizzo, get ready to take over."

"I've got it. I'll overtake on the ramp and slide into position," Rizzo said.

"Rizzo's car is departing the hotel. That's our guys. We'll catch up and then hang back to monitor."

Over the next twenty minutes, Frank followed the team's calls as they tracked the car to a café near the center of town. After the three men enjoyed a light meal, they returned to their vehicle and continued their drive without giving any indication they knew they were being followed.

Another fifteen minutes of driving, and the three arrived at an office building for the Lang Son Mining Company. After what appeared to be a quick conversation in the car, two of the men got out and entered the building. The driver exited a few minutes later, sat on the hood of the car, and lit a cigarette.

Forty-five minutes and three cigarettes later, the driver slipped his phone into his pocket and started the car back up as the two men emerged from the building.

"Heads up, looks like we're on the move again," Rizzo said.

An hour later, after a short stop at a cell-phone store, the blue Toyota rolled back into the Hotel del Luna parking lot. The men got out of the vehicle and went inside.

"I'm not sure if this is going to be it for the evening, fellas, so stay ready in case they decide to go out again once the sun goes down," Rizzo said.

Frank looked at Mike. "So, they eat, go talk to someone in an office building, get a cell phone, and come back. What are they up to? Think they're done for the night?"

"I'm not sure," Mike admitted. "But I think we have a couple of plays that might help. For starters, we should try to tag the vehicle. I hate not having a backup eye in the sky. Second, depending on how froggy SOCPAC wants to get, we could try to do some more active exploration. See if Ortiz here can get into the hotel's Wi-Fi network and poke around."

"Good idea. I'll hit up the watch officer and see what they say," Frank said. Picking up his laptop and headset, he moved to one of the bedrooms to make the call.

"That was quick," Mike said, looking at his watch, when Frank returned a few minutes later.

"The admiral happened to be standing next to the watch officer when I called. Helps to cut out the middleman. He approved the tag, but wasn't ready to do anything cyber related until we had some more information. Makes sense since he would have to run it up to General Cantrell for approval anyways. Cyber authorities are a bureaucratic nightmare."

"Everybody's got a boss. Even admirals," Mike mused. "Eli, prep one of our tags. LT, who do you want from your team to emplace it? Harder to explain an American poking around late at night."

"I agree with your assessment, Chief Smith. I will have them report to Sergeant Montgomery for system familiarization."

Over the next few hours, Frank and his team talked through the tag emplacement and prepared for their shift. At eleven p.m., they left the house and moved to replace Rizzo's team, repeating the process from earlier in the day.

"Have a good night, gentlemen," Rizzo said as his team pulled out of the area.

Frank and his team spent the next hour watching the empty streets. "All right, LT," he said, "let's get it done."

One of the Vietnamese Rangers got out of his vehicle and set up to provide close-in warning along the path a pedestrian would most likely take through the area. Thirty seconds later, a second Ranger walked into the parking lot and disappeared beside the blue Toyota. Ten seconds after that, he reappeared and continued walking around the building and down the block before circling back to his car.

Eli opened a connection through his phone to the tagging server and waited. "Got it, sir. Strong signal, full battery."

Frank keyed the radio. "Good work, guys. Definitely a win for us tonight."

Just before the sun came up, Mike's team came on station, and Frank headed back to the house. He hoped that the Chinese men were late risers so that he could get a shower and close his eyes for a few hours until they started stirring again. Lying down on the bed, he wondered what Kathy and Kyra were up to, but didn't even have time to finish the thought before he fell asleep.

-

Frank sat at the table staring at the laptop screen, waiting for the connection with SOCPAC to open. Mike occupied the chair next to him, just outside the camera's field of view. Frank straightened up as the connection went live and Admiral Jennings appeared at the head of his conference table.

"Good morning, sir. This is Captain Gonzales. Can you hear and see me OK?"

"Yes, I have you just fine, Captain. Good morning. It sounds like you all have been busy for the last several days. I've read your daily reports, but how about giving me a rundown?"

"Yes, sir. We received the initial report about the possible incursion four days ago, and sent teams to the two places my fox, Sergeant Wolters, assessed as the most likely for them to go: Cao Bang and Lang Son. We found them in Lang Son and set up a follow. After the first day, we emplaced a GPS tag to track them that way as well. Since then, we've maintained positive control of the three individuals the entire time. You see their exact movements laid out in our daily SITREPS, but their pattern of life holds fairly consistent. They move around between their hotel, local cafes and restaurants, and an occasional side stop at a cell-phone store or market. The biggest thing is what appears to be meetings with several mining corporations both at their headquarters and at several active mines. I have my Vietnamese Ranger counterpart, Lieutenant Nguyen, checking to see what we can find out about the nature of these meetings. The main anomaly in all of this is that they have often deviated significantly from the most direct route to some of these facilities. Some of those routes would be key lines of communication should the Chinese decide to invade from the east. They could very likely be using the mining thing as a cover to get them around."

"That could be," the admiral replied, "or they are actually interested in the mining industry. The Chinese have been extremely active in attempting to gain control over Vietnamese mining operation for the rare-earth-mineral deposits they have recently discovered. Given the pattern you described, that seems far more likely than some advanced reconnaissance for an impending invasion, don't you think?"

"That is what it looks like on the surface, sir," Frank agreed, "but there is something that doesn't sit right about this group and that story. We haven't been able to pinpoint exactly what it is yet, but there is something off."

"Well, let me help you with that, Captain," Admiral Jennings said. "I've got another report on my desk that says these visits aren't cordial business meetings. Instead, these three are doling out threats to these mining companies and issuing ultimatums should they decide not to start doing business with China."

"Sir, that would appear to make sense. Still, I think it's worth continuing to watch these guys until they head back across the border."

"No, Captain Gonzales, that won't be necessary. If we continue down this road, we run the risk of them finding out, if they haven't already. And then we'll have to deal with the bad press of harassing innocent businessmen in their own backyards. This isn't just coming from me. After the INDOPACOM commander's huddle this morning, I spoke with Admiral Lock about this. He made it clear, when he handed me that intel report, that we were to cease operations. I'm not going to be the one explaining an international incident to him or to Washington. Your team is to pull out and return to complete your training mission."

"Sir, if you're worried about exposure, we can use the GPS for tracking and continue to monitor in a more passive status. It wouldn't take any more resources, and that would significantly reduce the risk."

"No. I get that you want to keep working on this, but I am shutting it down. Pull your team back from Lang Son tonight." The admiral's tone hardened slightly, making it clear to Frank that there was no room for discussion.

"Yes, sir. We'll report in once we've closed this site down."

"Good work, Frank," Admiral Jennings said. "Sometimes we just hit dry holes. Probably better anyways, since the alternative would mean the Chinese might actually be trying to invade. Tell your team thanks for everything they are doing out there."

The connection severed, and Frank tossed his headphones onto the table. "Well, shit. Call the team in, Mike. The admiral just shut us down. He doesn't want to keep chasing ghosts."

"There's always more to the story when you get up to that level. No one likes chasing ghosts, but it gets way worse when you start playing the political game. The team did a hell of a job executing, though," Mike said, reaching for the radio. "All right, boys, go ahead and break off. Head back to the compound at Bac Kan. We'll close out the house and meet you there. Admiral's orders."

Frank knew the SOCPAC commander was right: that the three Chinese men were not paving the way for an invasion was what they wanted. On another positive note, not going to war with China meant that he would get back home to Kathy on schedule.

Chapter 9

"Well, look who the cat dragged in," Drew said, looking up from her cereal bowl as the door to the apartment opened.

Ish shuffled through the door and fell onto the couch. Drew had seen him exhausted before during finals, but there was an extra layer of sadness on his face that gave her pause.

"How are you holding up?" she asked, finally breaking the silence.

"I'm OK," he said. "It's just a lot. My family is a lot. He's gone, you know? He's the one who bought me my first computer when I was six. I used to sneak into his workshop late at night after my mom put me to bed. He would wave me over and carefully explain whatever electronics project he was working on."

"He also helped us both squeak by in our data-structures-and-algorithms class," Drew offered. "We thought we were being so sly with how we coaxed the answers out of him, but I'm pretty sure he knew. He was a great man, and I'm really sorry for your loss."

"Yeah, thanks. I'm going to go take a shower and try to sleep. I called Rich on my way back and told him I'd be in tomorrow. He was really understanding with giving me the space to take care of this."

Ish peeled himself off the couch and trudged down the hall toward his room. Drew had never seen him this way. She wished she had insisted on being there in person to support her friend over the last week. Although she couldn't change the past, Drew resolved to be there for him now, whether he thought he needed it or not.

The next morning, Drew and Ish walked into work together. Although he was still not himself, Drew was grateful to have her friend back.

"Coffee? You're buying," she said as they walked into the lobby.

"Always. The bad part about going home is that I'm the only coffee drinker in my family. Tea is not the same, and, like our founding fathers firmly believed, it is a reason to go to war."

"A reason for treason," Drew added with a laugh.

"See, folks," Ish said, appealing to an imaginary audience, "this girl gets it. She doesn't get a lot, but she gets this."

"Just for that, I'm getting an extra shot of espresso. Keep it up and I might get a scone as well."

"You wouldn't dare," Ish replied.

"And a fruit cup."

"Jeez, Lord Vader, I pray you don't alter this deal any further."

With coffee in hand, the two made their way upstairs. Drew opened the door to their office and held it open with an exaggerated flourish. "Ladies and gentlemen, the prodigal son has returned," she said loudly enough to carry past all of the cubicles.

It took Ish ten minutes to make it to his desk twenty feet away as everyone took turns to greet him and give their condolences. Drew circumvented the commotion and settled into her desk. After a quick scan of her email for any outstanding tasks, she looked over to find Ish at his desk. It was great to have him back.

"Have you guys seen the latest from China's drone program?" Randy asked over his shoulder to Drew and Ish. "Come check this out."

The two interns walked to Randy's desk and stood over him as he replayed the video. A Chinese reporter appeared to be standing at the edge of an open field with thick woods in the background.

Today marks another major achievement for the People's Republic of China and our army. General Xiang announced the creation of an entirely new operating methodology, bringing together the might of the Chinese people with the advancements we have made in advanced robotics. Man and machine will fight hand in hand as the new Veiled Dragon autonomous fighting vehicle becomes fully operational. General Xiang said that the People's Liberation Army will begin creating an entirely new division that integrates both human soldiers and Veiled Dragons down to the squad level, ushering in a new era of combat doctrine.

The reporter lowered her microphone slightly as the shot zoomed out. In the background, the camera began to pick up movement. Slowly, three soldiers in full battle gear began to emerge. Behind them, four tracked vehicles rolled into view. Each one looked to have machine guns mounted on an articulating arm. As soon as the drones rolled out of the clearing, the entire unit opened fire in unison. The three soldiers dropped into a prone position while the four vehicles raced ahead. Rushing past the reporter, who looked like she was doing her best not to appear frightened at the sudden burst of violence, the drones raced toward the camera.

The video cut to a different camera shot that showed a

small building. The drones rolled through the open field and spread out around the building while continuing to fire. Once they had set up in a semicircle around the building, the soldiers popped up and began running toward it. The drones continued firing even as the soldiers raced past them and rushed into the open door. From outside the building, the camera caught the muzzle flashes of the soldier's rifles. Ten seconds later, the soldiers emerged from the house and crouched along the front wall. The drones rolled past the structure while firing at another target off-screen. Once the drones had moved out of the frame, the soldiers stood up and ran in the same direction, leaving only a bullet-riddled building in view before the video cut back to the reporter.

General Xiang promised that this new division would be ready to fight for the people within the next year, and gave notice to the rest of the world that a stronger China was on the horizon.

As she finished her narration, a large quadcopter swooped in overhead, stopping directly above the reporter and pointed its guns at the camera. After a small pause for dramatic effect, the video cut out.

"That's some grade-A propaganda right there, huh?" Randy said, turning around in his chair.

"Why didn't the robots just do the whole thing? Why did the people have to go into the building first? Wouldn't it have made more sense for robots to do that dangerous part too?" Drew asked.

"Stop thinking like a logical American," Randy replied. "This is about propaganda and storytelling. Man and machine— together! Their actions don't have to make sense if it looks cool on film. Plus, the Chinese don't view their soldiers the same way that we do. They aren't going to just wantonly decimate their own forces, but killing a few conscripts won't make a general lose any sleep at night. Probably easier to explain than losing one of those fancy new dragon drones."

"I think it's really cool seeing what the future of warfare might become," Ish said. "I'm pretty sure we have something similar, if not better, lurking in a lab somewhere. There is something to be said about how powerful a force like that could be."

"Now link that with our project. New human-machine army being orchestrated by an advanced decision-making AI. That would be wild," Randy said.

"You know they have to be making one just like we are," Drew said.

"You'd be a fool to think they aren't," Randy said. "The Chinese have been just as interested in AI development as we have. And they've also been more eager to adopt it. It may be ego talking, but I don't think they have an AI as good as ours. I know you two haven't been on the project long, so you didn't see some of the high-end simulations we ran a few months back. It out-thought and outperformed every algorithm and human we pitted it against. It was beautiful. Going to be even more so when we can actually do it during an exercise with real soldiers."

"Beth doesn't seem to think the Army will go for a large-scale test," Drew said. "She seems to think they are too concerned about how it would be perceived from an ethical standpoint to put an AI in charge. Also, a job-security thing. Apparently, the generals are worried that an AI is coming for their positions."

"Maybe. But it would still be amazing to see," Randy said.

"That seems pretty shortsighted if you ask me," Ish said. "Why would an army not use every tool to their advantage?

I don't think I would like to fight as a part of an army that was knowingly making it riskier for me. That's the great thing about AI. It makes the world safer. Like nukes. If we make it known not only that we have the best equipment but that the head of our armies makes Napoleon look like an idiot, people will think twice before fighting us."

"That's one way to look at it," Randy admitted. "A new age of deterrence based on the overwhelming horror of what a full-scale war would look like. For that to be believable, though, we would have to see one actually out in the wild. It took two atomic bombs for the world to figure out how bad those were. I'm not sure the human in me wants to see that."

"Well, thankfully we work for the good guys, so we don't have to worry about our program being used to prove this point," Drew added. "Not to change the subject, but absolutely changing the subject, we should all go out to celebrate Ish coming back to us."

"An excuse to go out? With my fellow nerds? Count me in," Randy said.

"What do you think, Ish? I'm buying," Drew said before quickly adding, "*His* drinks, Randy. Just *his* drinks. I'm an intern after all."

"Darn. I was this close!" Randy said, measuring out a tiny distance with his finger and thumb.

"Yeah, OK. I'm going to go check in with my mom to see how she's doing now that most of the family has left," Ish said as he walked toward the office entrance.

"I can't believe you left the 'asking Mom's permission to go out' ribbing opportunity on the table," Randy said to Drew.

"I suppose I'm rising to new levels of maturity," Drew said. "He'll get a pass for a few, but I can only keep the kid gloves on for so long."

"Your magnanimity is boundless."

"Oh no, it definitely has bounds. He won't be safe forever," Drew grinned. "But now I'm off to tell the others about our soiree."

Drew spent the rest of the day recruiting people for drinks that evening and asking Beth to walk her through the changes Beth had recently made to some of the project's code. Although interns were encouraged to engage with the full-time staff to learn everything they could, Drew marveled at her complete lack of productivity when she looked at the clock on the wall and saw that it was already four forty-five.

"Guess what time it is!" Drew drummed on Ish's desk.

"Super-annoying friend time?"

"It's time to make like a tree and get the eff out of here! I'm going to start rounding up the usual suspects."

"Oh, yeah, drinks."

"What do you mean, 'Oh, yeah, drinks'? I'm going to need a little more enthusiasm."

"My enthusiasm is hard to spot through the ruggedly handsome exterior you see before you."

"Nothing about you says 'ruggedly handsome.' More like above-average nerd who is going to make some lucky lady very happy one day. If, that is, he can pull himself together."

"OK, OK. I'm just trying to dig myself out of the hole I'm in from being out of the office for a week. Let me do one or two more things and then I'll meet you there. Pretend it's a surprise party or something, and when I get there, I'll act really surprised."

"Fine. Just don't go sneaking off again." Drew pushed herself off Ish's chair, causing him to spin, and rounded up the rest of the team.

Having set up shop in the corner of their usual pub, Drew returned from the bar with two ciders. She passed one to Beth and slid into the booth.

"Do you think I should try to sign on with DARPA permanently?" Drew asked. Since Drew had joined the team, Beth had become one of her closest mentors.

"You could certainly do worse. The good thing about being here is that we aren't subject to the same profit-driven deadlines as our counterparts out in the corporate world. Sure, we still have timelines and due dates, but it just isn't the same. It's far closer to getting to actually explore and see where the science takes you. I think that's magical, but at the same time I'm not sure if I would have fully appreciated it if I hadn't spent time out in the real world. On the other hand, if you find a company that is doing something truly unique and interesting, you have more of an opportunity to leave your lasting mark on society."

"That's kind of what I figured you would say. I just don't see the same allure to the startup culture that everyone else from my graduating class saw. I think what we are working on could still have those same society-shifting ramifications. Plus, sometimes you run across super-interesting people."

"Honestly, as long as you don't stay here because you think it's the safe option, then I will be happy for you. And anywhere you decide to land will be lucky to have you."

The two women continued talking as more people trickled in. Although Drew was closer to Beth than to any of the others, the entire team had taken to both of the interns, and the conversation swelled as people gave their opinions, offering to connect Drew to friends and colleagues, and generally falling over themselves to help the new graduates become successful. Wrapped in the conversation, Drew didn't notice the time until the end of her third cider.

"It's seven already? Where's Ish?"

"I don't think he's come in yet," Henry said. "I was one of the last ones to leave the office, and he was still going strong when I walked out."

"He'd better not miss his own party!" Drew opened the messenger app on her phone. *Ish, c'mon man, you're not going to stand me up again, are you? Everyone is wondering where you are!*

Sorry! 5 more minutes and I'm out of here, he replied.

"Maybe this was a bad idea," Drew said. "In college he was usually the first one at the bar. Was this pushing it for him? I thought it would help get his mind off of his grandfather and feel normal again."

"It's possible, but that's OK," Randy said. "You've done nothing wrong. Besides, even if he's going to miss most of the party, the rest of us are glad you got us all out."

Drew sat back in the booth and listened as the rest of the team carried on in their usual mode of conversation, bouncing among four or five subjects that would provoke despair in any uninitiated listener who tried to. As she flicked the rim of her glass, Drew's mind slowly wandered away from the conversation and back to the look on Ish's face when he walked into their apartment last night.

"I'm going to go get him. Not sure if we'll come back here or if we'll just head home for the night."

"OK. Well, let us know either way so we don't worry about you," Beth said, leaning over and giving Drew a hug.

"Yes, Mother," Drew said with an eye roll.

She grabbed her bag and slid out of the booth before making her way through the crowded bar and out onto the street.

Walking into the half-lit lobby of the office, she pushed the button to the elevator and rode it up to her floor.

"Ish, I've come to put a stop to your productivity!" she shouted as she got off the elevator. "You'd better save whatever you have open, because I'm going to shut it down."

Rounding the corner to their cubicle, Drew saw that Ish's desk was unoccupied, and his bag was gone.

Where are you? I'm at the office, and you're not here. If you didn't want to come out, you could have just said something. I'm coming home and we can talk. No need to be around everyone else.

Drew returned her phone to her pocket and walked back out of the building toward her apartment. Checking her phone every couple of minutes to see if Ish had messaged, she started to get agitated. It was one thing to blow off a meetup, but another thing entirely to not text her back. And this was the second time. She sensed that something was off, and that feeling was made even stronger when she opened the door to their apartment and was greeted by a darkened interior with no signs of Ish.

Starting to panic, she pulled her phone out and found the contact for Ish's mother.

"Hello?" came a voice on the other end.

"Hi, Mrs. Tilley? This is Drew Drum, Ish's friend."

"Oh, hi, Drew!" Mrs. Tilley said warmly, "It's great to hear from you."

"I'm trying to find Ish. He blew off an after-work thing, and isn't at home. I was wondering if he mentioned anything to you when he called you earlier."

"Called me? No, I haven't talked to Ish since he left here

yesterday afternoon. Is everything all right?"

"Yesterday afternoon? He didn't call you around lunch today?" Drew asked.

"No, and I don't have any missed calls. Is there something I need to be worried about?"

"It's probably nothing. Maybe he just needed some space to deal with his grandfather's death. Thank you, Mrs. Tilley."

"What do you mean? His grandfather isn't dead. He's out playing golf with his friends as we speak."

"Well, I, uh. . . I must have misunderstood him the other day," Drew stammered, "I'm relieved that he's all right."

"Are you sure everything is OK, Drew?" she asked.

"Oh, yeah, I'm sure everything will be ok. Thank you again."

"You're most welcome, dear. If I hear from him, I'll make sure he gives you a call."

"Thanks. Good night."

"OK, Ish, what the hell?" Drew said aloud to the empty apartment. "Where did you run off to?"

Chapter 10

"So that's it, sir," Matt said. "Unless we can get one of these systems and take it apart in a lab, we won't be able to confirm what it does or what its capabilities are. But based on all the evidence we have, it's likely China now has a device that can instantly decrypt any communication as long as it's within a certain range. What that range is we don't know, and we don't know exactly what the lifespan of the system is before it fails, just that it's around a week. The only good news is that we can spot its signature through its massive power consumption, but even then we don't have the resources to constantly search everywhere for one coming online. We have to rely on some other cue to know to look for it." Matt looked to his left to see if Colonel Banks would pick up the conversation or wait for General Cantrell to respond.

"That's good work, Major Anderson," the general said. "As much as I don't want your conclusion to be correct, it fits and is the best working theory we have. If you're right, then not only are we lagging way behind in our technological development, but we're also at an absolutely catastrophic disadvantage in any competition we get into with the Chinese."

The general stared at the world map on the wall of the conference room. "JB, do your folks have any sort of indication on how many of these things they have in the inventory, how long it takes to make them, that sort of thing?"

Colonel Banks paused. "Sir, we don't have much to go on with that, because we just don't have the ability to produce it ourselves. Our best guess is that the neodymium is the limiting factor in the whole thing, because that's most of what the core seems to be made of. It's also one of the main minerals that China seems to be going after in their mining acquisitions over the past couple of years, which is weird, because at one point they were one of the largest miners and exporters of the element in the world. If that's the case, then they seem to be running out of their own stockpiles, or at least can't get it out of the ground fast enough."

"How are we so blind here?" General Cantrell asked.

"Sir, we just got beat on this. We are so far behind that it's going to take us a long time to catch up. Best case is for us to find a unit intact and reverse engineer one."

"All right. I've got my meeting with the secretary tomorrow afternoon to talk about China's saber-rattling in Vietnam, so I'll let him know what you dug up, and where you think we are with this. He's not going to be happy and is going to be looking for options. Find me some options. Find out where it's being made, where it's going to be used, how we stop it. Something. I'm pretty sure I don't have to preach to you two about how bad this is if we can't counter it."

Everyone in the conference stood as General Cantrell rose and walked out of the conference room.

"Sir, he knows that we don't have the placement, access, or subject-matter expertise to answer any of those questions, right?" Matt asked as he and Colonel Banks made their way out of the headquarters building. "I mean, I don't really even know where to start with that."

"Of course he does," Colonel Banks replied, "but who the hell else is he going to ask? He's not looking to me because we have a team of subject-matter experts on this particular topic on hand. He's looking to the unit because we're good at coming up with ways to find answers to hard problems and generating options for him and senior leaders to solve them. And the unit is good at that, because we bring in people like you. You say you don't know where to start, but you do. Start with where you are, and take a single step that gets you in the right direction. And then take another. You might hit a dead end and have to backtrack a little bit, but I've seen your work both before you got here and during the training pipeline. You'll find out where you're going eventually."

Matt knew the colonel was telling him what he needed to hear, and he was a little mad at himself that it was working. He would find a way, because if he didn't, it was likely no one would.

-

Twenty-two messages, eight calls to Ish's phone, two calls to the police, and two more to Mrs. Tilley. Drew was running out of options and starting to panic. When he hadn't shown up to happy hour, she'd figured that he had just landed a last-minute date with a girl from a dating app, but then he didn't come back to the apartment the next day or the day after. It wasn't just her he was ghosting, either. Mrs. Tilley had tried several times with no luck. The police hadn't been helpful either, mistaking Drew for a crazy ex-girlfriend bent on harassing Ish. Before hanging up, the officer had all but accused Drew of stalking.

They weren't going to be any help, at least for a few more days.

Until then, she was on her own, and the fact that he had totally fallen off the face of the Earth made Drew more and more certain that Ish was in some kind of trouble. Walking across the apartment, she opened the door to Ish's room. Although they'd been roommates since their last year in college, Drew had never actually gone into Ish's room before. She treated it as the physical manifestation of the line in their relationship she didn't want to cross for fear of ruining their friendship, but all of that didn't matter if he was in trouble.

Stepping over the pile of laundry on the floor, she sat down at Ish's desk and turned on his computer. Although it had a password on the lock screen, she knew enough about her best friend that she guessed his password on the third attempt. She didn't know what she was looking for, but opened an internet browser to his email. There were a dozen unread emails waiting for him, starting on the night he disappeared, so it didn't look like he had checked it since then.

She scrolled down through the inbox to the emails from before he'd left, but they also didn't yield anything of value. His Reddit account was also useless, although some of the subreddits he subscribed to made her remember why she had never wanted to snoop around in his computer before. Opening the file browser, she looked through his recent documents, downloads, photos, and the folders on his desktop. Nothing.

Drew gave up looking on the laptop and started rifling through the desk drawers. Buried underneath pens and takeout menus, was an external hard drive in the back corner of one of the drawers. With a little more digging, she found the USB cable and connected it to the computer. Once it registered, a password window appeared. Drew input the same password that had logged her on to the desktop, but it was incorrect. *You have 9 attempts remaining*, the window warned. She tried two other passwords, but decided not to push her luck.

"What did you put on here that you don't want anyone to see?" Drew said aloud. Reopening the browser, she clicked on the download history. Mixed with memes and other random documents she had already found during her first look through the computer were several zip files he had downloaded to an external device. Two were dated the day before Ish went missing. "What are you?" Drew muttered. "Ish, what are these?"

Although she had a feeling that whatever was on the hard drive might be important, she was stuck once again, because she had no way to access what was on it. Drew pushed herself back from the desk and slowly spun the chair in circles while trying to figure out her next course of action. Then she remembered the guy from the coffee shop. If he was who she thought he was, he might be able to help her. Getting up from the chair, she put her shoes on and headed for the office.

Stepping onto the elevator, she had to consciously stop herself from hitting the button for the third floor, and instead pushed five.

"Dr. Nascent?" she asked, standing at the edge of the open office.

"Yes, can I help you?" he replied.

"Hi, I'm Drew Drum. I work downstairs with Dr. Long. I'm one of his interns."

"Oh, hello, come in, please," Dr. Nascent said, motioning to a seat in front of his desk. "How are you liking the internship?

Is it what you were expecting?"

"It has been amazing. I've learned so much just by being around the project and watching what everyone else has been doing. Plus, Beth Somersby has taken me under her wing. I really couldn't have asked for a better introduction to DARPA or life outside of college."

"That's wonderful. Do you think we might be able to keep you around? Or is the lure of Silicon Valley simply too tempting?"

"I'm still trying to figure that out. But I actually came here with another question for you. There was a guy here a little while ago. Matt something. Maybe six feet tall, brown hair? He said he was looking for you, but you were out, so he left a note on your door to call him back."

"Oh yes, I remember him. Is there something wrong?"

"No, nothing bad. He and I talked in the coffee shop downstairs for a while, and I had a couple of follow-up questions for him. Do you still have his number?"

"I think I do somewhere. Are you interested in a job with special operations forces? That would be very exciting work. Working with people like Matt on things like they do, not that I really know anything. Based on what little I found out from a fellow War College student who is over there, though, they are the real deal. The guys doing things in places that you and I will never know about," Dr. Nascent said as he searched through papers on his desk. "Ah. Here we go. Matt Anderson."

Drew watched as he copied the information onto a new piece of paper.

"Here you go. Stop by anytime. Once you get to be my age, you suddenly find yourself living vicariously through the up-and-coming folks." He folded the paper and handed it to her.

"Please give Matt my regards."

Drew thanked Dr. Nascent and slipped the piece of paper into her pocket and walked back into the hall. Finding an empty office, she shut the door and dialed the number on the paper.

"Hello?" came a voice on the other end.

"Hello, my name is Drew Drum. I'm trying to reach Matt Anderson."

"This is Matt."

"Hi," Drew said, wishing she had taken the time to come up with what she was going to say. "I'm not sure if you remember me. We met in the coffee shop at DARPA."

"Oh, sure. Hi, Drew. I don't remember giving you my number, though."

"Yeah," she said, suddenly unsure whether she should have called him, "Dr. Nascent gave it to me. I hope that's all right?"

"It's fine. What can I help you with, Drew Drum from DARPA?"

"Well, I have a problem that I think you might be able to help me with. It's a little hard to explain over the phone. My friend that ran into you. He's gone missing, and I haven't been able to get a hold of him for days, which is really unlike him. Even before this, he had been acting weird. I don't know how to describe it, but now that I'm looking back on it there was just something maybe off. Or maybe I'm in my head."

"So how can I help?" Matt interrupted.

Thankful that he had stopped her from continuing to ramble, Drew continued, "Right. Well, I found a hard drive that he may have downloaded some zip files onto, but it's locked and I can't get into it."

"You know it's probably just porn, right?"

"Gross, no. Ish wouldn't bother to put a bunch of security for that stuff anyways, I don't think. At least not the amount that would be on this hard drive—and why encrypt a drive? If it's some of that weird stuff, maybe it's still related?"

"This is really eating at you, isn't it?" Matt asked.

"I just want to know my friend isn't in trouble."

"Well, I suppose I do owe you one for looking at those schematics. Tell you what, give me your address and I'll stop by and take a look. Once we figure out that it's just a collection of photos of ladies' feet or something, you can stop worrying about it. Does that work?"

"Yes, thank you. I'll text you the address," Drew said.

"Great. I'll let you know when I'm on my way," Matt said and disconnected.

As she typed the address to her apartment into a text message to Matt, Drew tried not to feel ridiculous for how she must have just sounded on the phone.

-

Drew opened the door to the apartment and motioned for Matt to come in.

"Thanks for coming over. I hope it's not too much of an inconvenience," she said, walking him through the living room to the table next to the kitchen.

"It's OK. You sounded pretty stressed on the phone. I'm not sure I'm going to actually be able to help you with anything, but at least I might be able to rule this out as a possible lead," Matt said as he slipped off his bag and set it next to the laptop and hard drive on the table. Sitting down, Matt pressed the space bar to wake up the laptop. "Do you have the password for his Windows account?"

"Oh yeah, it's *one ring to rule them all*—one word, all lower-case."

"Nice," Matt said as the computer finished loading. He reached into his bag and removed a device that looked to Drew like another external hard drive with a small screen and a few extra buttons. Fishing out a cable, Matt connected the device to the laptop and waited. After a few seconds, a command-prompt window opened, and Matt began typing.

"Could I get a glass of water?" he asked without looking up.

"Sure," Drew said. Moving into the kitchen, she pulled a glass down from the shelf and filled it with water. She set it down on the table, and then leaned back on the kitchen counter, watching him type. Although she desperately wanted to know what that device was and what he was doing, she did her best to resist standing over Matt's shoulder.

Drew looked up from the Reddit feed on her phone when she saw the screen light up as a new window appeared over the black background of the command prompt.

"Big *Lord of the Rings* fan then, was he?" Matt asked. "First *one ring to rule them all*, and now this one was *speak friend and enter*."

"Really? I tried that," Drew said, with a hint of disappointment.

"Sorry, it's *speak friend and*; then you hit the Enter key," Matt clarified. "Pretty clever."

"Well, at least I was close. What's on it?"

"Let's take a look," Matt said as he clicked to open the first zip file. "This one was last modified three days ago. Looks like there's a text file in it. Little odd to compress that."

Please proceed with the plan. We will meet at our usual place in the park at 8:00.

"What?" Drew said. "That's what it says?"

Matt didn't answer, but clicked on the next file, which contained another single text document.

Please prepare to execute the plan. We will follow with more details.

We are excited to hear that the test file executed successfully. Please bring the drive with you when next we meet.

We are happy to hear of your new position, and would like to speak with you more. We will meet tomorrow at 1 a.m.

Matt stopped after this message, and looked over his shoulder at Drew. "I'm not going to open any more of these here, because I think you and I both know where this is going."

The blood drained from Drew's face at the realization of what these files implied. She opened her mouth to speak, but no words came. Her friend—her closest friend for going on five years—was a spy? Was he capable of that? How had this happened? When? Who was he working for? Drew had a thousand questions, and looking at Matt, she wasn't sure if she would ever learn the answers to any of them. Tears streamed down her face.

Matt rose out of the chair and turned to hug her. He had so many questions running through his mind, but couldn't begin to imagine what this young woman must be going through. He wrapped his arms around her and pulled her into his chest. After a moment, he caught movement on the screen. The cursor was moving on its own, and the light next to the webcam was illuminated.

"Don't move, and don't say anything," Matt whispered to Drew. "Someone has remotely accessed that computer and activated the webcam."

Matt strained to see the screen in the reflection off the microwave door without turning his face to the camera. As he did, he saw the cursor select all the documents and delete them. The progress window popped up, and the completion bar began to fill. Keeping his back turned to the computer, Matt reached back, slammed the lid of the laptop closed, and unplugged the external drives. He wasn't sure how much they had seen or how much they'd been able to erase before the connection was severed. Matt flipped the laptop over and removed the battery. He shoved everything into his bag.

"I don't know what we've just stumbled into, but it's not good. If your friend was really working with someone who has access and controls like this in place, then you're potentially in some serious trouble. I don't know if they got a good look at either of us, but I'm willing to bet they already know all about you."

"What do you mean they know all about me? Why? Because I live with him? What does that matter?"

"These are all great questions, but we don't have time for that right now. If there is something serious enough on this drive, then they might be willing to take additional steps to keep whatever's on it from getting out. We need to leave right now."

"I don't—"

"Right now," Matt interrupted. He slung his bag over his shoulder. "If you want to grab your phone, do it, but we should not be here."

Drew unplugged her phone from the charger on the kitchen counter and grabbed her purse. Matt moved to the front door of the apartment and cracked it open to look out into the hallway.

"All right, let's go. I'm probably just being paranoid, but it's better to err on the side of caution," he said, leading Drew out of the apartment and into the hallway. Locking the door behind them, Drew put her keys in her purse and caught up to walk next to Matt to the elevator. Reaching for the button, Matt stopped short as the chime rang to indicate a car stopping on their level.

As the doors parted, Matt started to enter, but stopped when he saw three men in the center of the car. Matt's eyes locked in with the man in the middle, who flashed a look of recognition. After a brief moment of shock, the man reached for his belt line and started drawing a pistol. Matt pivoted off his front leg and drove a push kick straight into the man's chest, sending him tumbling backward into his two companions. With that momentary head start, Matt turned around, grabbed Drew by the hand, and ran toward the stairwell they had passed coming out of her apartment.

They were two flights down when he heard the door slam into the concrete wall as the three men sprinted after them. With three flights remaining, Matt wasn't sure if they would make it through the door and into the garage before their pursuers caught up to them. Two floors to go. The stairwell burst with sound as one of the men shot at them from the landing above. He missed to the right, and the time it took to stop and fire was just enough for Matt and Drew to push through the doorway and into the garage. Immediately to their right was a row of cars along the wall, and Matt dragged Drew behind a silver Prius. Crouching down, they watched as the three men ran out into the garage. The men stopped, looking for signs of their quarry, and one of them directed the other two down one row while he started running along a parallel one.

Matt wasn't sure if his ruse would work, but he quietly moved out from behind the parked car and grabbed the door just before it closed. Holding it open, he motioned to Drew, who went back into the stairwell. Matt followed, and then moved past her to the door on the opposite end of the well that led out to the street. Once outside, the two raced across the street, narrowly missing a delivery truck, and disappeared down an alley. They continued to run for another block before Matt slowed his pace to a walk.

"Are you OK?" he asked.

"No, I'm not OK. Who were they? Why did they shoot at us?" Drew said, trying to catch her breath.

"They are probably the same people that were alerted when we accessed that hard drive. My guess is that they had installed a trip wire onto Ish's machine that triggered when we started poking around in there. These were the guys sent to find out who was on the other end in case their remote wipe was unsuccessful."

"I don't understand."

"I know it's a lot to take in. Especially when you're still amped up from being chased by armed men. We're going to get you somewhere safe, and figure out what we can make of this thing, OK? I'm not going to let anything bad happen to you."

Drew stared at him for a long moment. "Who are you?"

"For now, I'm the guy who is getting you out of here. I'll explain more later. My car is one more block over, so we'll take that and put some distance between us and those guys. Sound good?"

Drew nodded and followed Matt to his car. The two sat in

silence for the twenty-minute drive to Matt's apartment, and Drew followed wordlessly as he led her up the stairs to his floor. Once inside, she sat down on the couch, and tried her best to keep the tears from welling up. Matt set his bag on the table, grabbed the box of tissues from the kitchen counter, and sat next to Drew. He handed a tissue to the young woman, who started drying her eyes.

"Ish gave them something important, didn't he?" she asked, staring at the floor.

"I don't know, but what we've found doesn't look good. Normal people don't keep messages about meetings and executing plans in text files on secure hard drives. They also don't have three Chinese operatives come to kill you when you look at their computer."

"You are what I think you are, aren't you?"

"That depends on what you think I am."

"You're a spy for the CIA."

"No, I don't work for the agency. I'm in the Army."

"So, you're an Army spy."

"Let's see what more we can find about what your friend was up to. I'm going to make a pot of coffee. Would you like some?"

"Yes, please, that would be great."

Drew watched as Matt went into the kitchen and started the coffee maker. Walking around to the table, he unpacked his bag, laying out his laptop, Ish's computer, the hard drive, and the device she had seen him connect to Ish's laptop earlier. He powered on his computer and connected the device.

"What is that?" she asked.

"It's a tool kit that has a bunch of programs to help me with technical exploitation and computer forensics. For example, it kept a log of the processes running on Ish's system and the traffic coming and going over the Wi-Fi interface."

"So you can go back through the logs to see whether there was some sort of trip-wire thing."

"Exactly. Here, come look at this," Matt said, pointing at the screen.

Drew came over from the couch and sat down at the table next to him.

"Sixty seconds after we logged in to the system using his username and password, there was a small burst of traffic that went out to an external IP address. Looking through what's loaded in his registry . . ." Matt trailed off for a moment. "There. That's the program that transmitted. It wasn't when we opened the hard drive. Whoever was handling Ish put this on his computer so that they would know whenever his system went active."

"Ish was a computer guy, though. He would have found that."

"Which means . . ."

"He knew it was there."

"Probably."

"Ish, what were you doing?" Drew asked aloud as the coffee maker began gurgling. She turned to Matt. "Where are your mugs?"

"Above the coffee maker." Matt pointed without looking up. "There's some milk in the refrigerator you can help yourself too. I'm a black-coffee kind of guy, though, so there's no cream or sugar in the place."

Drew poured the coffee into two cups, adding milk to hers. Returning to the table, she slid one across the table.

"Thanks," he said.

"You're welcome."

Matt continued looking through the log files. "Here's where the remote connection started. It looks like they took control through a program already installed on Ish's system, activated the webcam, and then started trying to delete the files from the hard drive."

"Can you see what was captured from the webcam?"

"Yeah, let me pull the file," Matt said, navigating to a different folder. The video player popped up and began running. The footage started right after Matt stood up to hug her, so the only thing visible was the living room and his back turned to the camera. The two watched as Matt leaned over to whisper into Drew's ear, and then his arm reached back toward the camera. The video cut off with the camera panning down to the floor as the laptop lid slammed shut.

Matt breathed a sigh of relief. "They don't get a good look at either of us, which is really lucky."

"That is so creepy. I mean, you hear about people activating webcams and spying on you, but it's totally different when you're the one actually in the video," Drew said. "Do you know where the connection originated?"

"Let's see what we can pull from the traffic data. Here's the IP address. Looks like they're trying to obscure it through a VPN. Looking at what came out from the VPN on the other side . . . registered here. Just across the river in Maryland. Pairing that IP to a physical address . . . someone from Xing Tao Logistics."

"Ish was working with the Chinese?"

"Those three gentlemen in the elevator certainly lend weight to that theory. Now that we know who was chasing us, let's see if we can find out what they were trying to keep us from finding," Matt said, picking up Ish's external drive and plugging it into his computer. "Crap," he said when the folder popped up.

"Where are all the files?" Drew asked.

"Looks like they managed to erase all of them. They may not be totally gone, though. I'll see if there's any that I can recover."

Matt opened his disk-recovery program and set it to run. While it processed the hard drive, he began a search on Xing Tao Logistics, pulling up the customer-facing website, financial documentation, firm-leadership profiles, and recent news releases. It all pointed to a legitimate company, but that was the point. One of the advantages the Chinese had was their ability to co-opt legitimate businesses for use in intelligence activities, and this firm seemed to be yet another example of that. Since the company's American headquarters sat just outside of Washington, DC, Matt guessed that the intelligence community was already aware of its after-hours activities, but just in case they weren't, he included its basic information in the incident report he was drafting on the day's events.

Matt's laptop chimed to let him know the recovery was complete. He clicked on the window and saw the small list of files. "Well, this definitely isn't all of the ones we saw earlier, and we can't see any metadata on when they were created. Let's try and piece together what we can." Opening each text file, Matt copied the one to two sentences into a single Word document.

We are excited to hear that the test file executed successfully. Please bring the drive with you when next we meet.

We are very glad you have decided to meet with us again. We think that this can be the start of a positive relationship.

We are pleased you have found our gift to your liking, and hope it will help with your studies.

We will meet at 8pm at our usual library reading room.

We are happy to hear of your new position, and would like to speak with you more. We will meet tomorrow at 1 a.m.

We will talk more about your find at our next meeting. If the program is as complete as you say, you may be the hero.

Sitting back, Matt and Drew stared at the messages.

"That's it?" Drew asked.

"That's what we've got. Of the hundreds on the drive, they got all but these six."

"If these are even remotely believable, my best friend has been working with Chinese agents since college. Maybe longer than I've even known him. He was the one who pushed so hard for us to go to DARPA. Was that at their direction? Did they plant him here to steal something from DARPA?"

"Insider threats are the best vector for people to get inside a network. They're supposed to be there, and nothing is out of the ordinary with them accessing information. We'll have to let DARPA's security and counterintelligence team know they need to do a scan of their systems to see what might have been compromised. What project were you assigned to? What was it that Ish gave them?"

"We were working on an advanced decision-making tool. Essentially, it was an AI military commander that could ingest all sorts of battlefield data and make decisions about how to employ units to beat the enemy."

"How far along were you in development?"

"It was done. Ish and I came on board to an already fully functioning model that had passed all sorts of training scenarios and had beaten every military force put against it. They even tried it with historical armies. It fought in ancient

Rome, Napoleonic Europe, Asia, World War I—it didn't matter. What Rich and the team had made was the most impressive thing. I was so honored to even be the silly intern. They were planning on doing some tests with real soldiers in training soon. That kept getting delayed, though, because the generals didn't trust the system."

"Turning over control to a machine is never going to sit well with anyone who has spent a day in the American military. It's just not how we think. You would have a riot on your hands up and down the chain of command if you gave robotic orders to commanders and didn't provide them the latitude to execute a mission as they saw fit. The Chinese PLA, on the other hand, already has a rigid command structure built on compliance and obedience. And now Ish has just given China an AI that they can put at the top of their military to perfectly orchestrate their operations. This isn't good. I'm going to package this up into my report and send it off to my unit."

Matt sat at his computer drafting the incident report. Drew quickly got bored of watching him type and got up. Pausing between thoughts, Matt looked over and saw Drew asleep on the couch. He pulled a blanket from the hall closet, laid it over the woman, and dimmed the lights. Returning to his computer, he finished his report and sent it to Colonel Banks. Eventually, he would have to figure out what to do with Drew and this latest case of Chinese espionage, but first Matt wanted to take a shower.

As he was drying off, his phone buzzed with an incoming message.

We found another one. Honolulu. 5 days old. -Dean

Matt put on a fresh set of clothes. Walking out into the living room, he gently shook Drew's shoulder. "Drew, wake up."

Drew sat up. "How long was I out?"

"An hour. Maybe a little more."

"Thank you for the blanket. And the nap. I needed that."

"You're welcome. We're going to Hawaii."

"Wait, what? I think I've missed something."

"Do you remember that design I had you look at? We found another one. It went active five days ago in Hawaii, which means I have two days to get there and try to recover it before it reaches its failure point. I have to go. I think you'll be safer there with me than you are here without me. Chances are good they've got a thick file with your name on it as an associate of their asset, Ish. Chances are also good that they believe you found the contents of that hard drive, so they're going to be looking for you. Plus, you seem to have a better understanding of this tech than I do, and that could be really helpful."

"OK."

"Good choice. Our flight leaves in ninety minutes, and there's an Uber five minutes out."

"What if I decide not to go?

"Then I will have misjudged you. If that's the case, I'll leave you with someone I know I can trust to keep you safe while we figure out what's going on. Is that what you want?"

"I've never been to Hawaii before."

Chapter 11

"Do you have a moment, Captain?" Lieutenant Nguyen asked with a knock on the open door.

"Of course, LT. What's up?" Frank said, getting up to greet his partner. Over the past two days, the two had done their best to return to the preplanned training schedule and mask their disappointment at being pulled from the surveillance mission. Frank had been spending more time at his desk instead of out at the range than he normally would have, and seeing the Vietnamese officer now made him feel guilty for distancing himself from the training.

"My unofficial inquiries into our three Chinese gentlemen have returned to me," the lieutenant said. "They did, in fact, meet with executives from several mining firms. According to people who were there, their tactics were quite aggressive, including making nearly overt threats against the executives themselves should they not give in to their demands."

"So, the admiral was right, then. It might be sketchy business practice, but they were there working an economic angle."

"On the surface, but that is not the entire report. The executives noted that these three individuals were not legitimate. They did not compose themselves like the experienced mining executives they claimed to be. There were inconsistencies in the way they spoke and their knowledge of the industry. They simply did not fit."

"How reliable is this?"

"I do not question the man who gave me this report. If he said it, it is an accurate assessment."

"You know as well as I do that if we open this back up and we are wrong, it's going to be very bad for both of us."

"And you know that if we are right, the ire of a bureaucrat is the least of our concerns."

Frank stared at the lieutenant, trying to decide whether this hunch was worth killing his career. What the hell, he thought, he was planning on getting out anyway. Frank cracked a smile. "You know, LT," he said, "the admiral ordered us off so quickly we didn't have time to retrieve our tag from the bottom of that Toyota. I wonder what it's been up to."

"Shall we look?"

Frank sat back down behind his computer and loaded the tracking interface. Blue dots began appearing on the map as the positioning data plotted on the screen. Using the time bar at the bottom, he went back to when the team had pulled off of the vehicle.

"OK. Here's the time when we lost our eyes on these guys," he said. "Let's see where they've been since we left." Frank slowly advanced the time bar. For several hours the icon didn't move, but then it left the hotel parking lot. At first, the vehicle maintained the same pattern of life Frank had become accustomed to seeing, making stops at a restaurant, two small shops in town, and a café. They watched as the icon made its way into the heart of the city.

"And now they're going back to harass some more mining executives," Frank said as the time continued to advance.

"No, something is unusual. Please add more detail to their location," Lieutenant Nguyen said.

Frank zoomed in. "Driving down the road."

"They are stopped on the side of the road. They are not moving, but the clock continues to advance."

Frank looked and saw that the lieutenant was right. For six minutes, the vehicle stopped on the side of the road. When it restarted, the icon reversed direction and began moving north.

"We've never seen that before either. They never pulled over, and never completely reversed course. What just happened?" Frank asked.

"We will see where they go from here, but my hypothesis is that they may have just received a phone call and are now forging a different path."

Frank and Lieutenant Nguyen watched as the vehicle left Lang Son and continued driving north. It paused again for ten minutes in Dong Dang before resuming its course until it reached the town of Ta Lung, near the border with China. The icon sat idle for ten minutes close to the border, and then reversed course back south.

For the next fifteen minutes, Frank and Lieutenant Nguyen watched the icon's movements unfold, accounting for the time since the team had stopped their surveillance. When the time scale reached the present, the two men sat in silence.

"What was that? Why did they just go on a driving tour of the province?" Frank finally asked.

"I am unsure. It does not appear to conform to any pattern of these so-called mining executives."

"I'm hungry, and I bet the boys are tired of being out at the range," Frank said, standing up from his chair. "Didn't you say there was a really good place up north of here for dinner?"

Lieutenant Nguyen stared at Frank for a moment, and then realization washed over the lieutenant's face. "Yes, in fact, there is a fantastic place in Ta Lung. I believe that our soldiers would be very happy for a drive and to eat there."

Frank and the lieutenant drove out to the range where the Green Berets and Rangers were working on weapon-transition drills.

"Chief!" Frank yelled. "Grab Sergeant Tran and come over here."

"Hey, sir, what's up?"

"Chief, the LT and I are so pleased with this fine-quality training that we are going to treat you all to dinner. Isn't that right, Lieutenant?"

"You are correct, Captain. There is a wonderful place I have heard about near Ta Lung."

"Ta Lung? That's like four hours . . ." Mike stopped mid-sentence as he caught on to what Frank was saying. "Sir, that sounds excellent. I've heard that area is absolutely stunning. Should we bring the camera and binoculars too?"

"Chief, that's an outstanding idea. Have the guys bring whatever they'd like to take in all the sights."

An hour later, the ODA and six Vietnamese Rangers drove out of the compound and headed north. While en route, Dave and Rizzo segmented out the tracking device's positioning data so that the team could split into three groups to drive the routes identified in the data log. Arriving just after sunset, the team found a small restaurant to eat at, refueled their vehicles, and set out along their assigned routes.

Frank set the GPS on the dashboard so that both Tim and he could see it, and watched as Tim drove south along the border. As they went, the team mirrored each stop for the same duration shown in the tag's data file. First at a major intersection, then a bridge, followed by a small village. At each location, the team took photos and quickly assessed the situation before moving on. By midnight, the team arrived at the outskirts of Lang Son, and by two thirty a.m. they had reached the outskirts of Hanoi. Just before sunrise, Tim rolled to a stop back at the small compound in Bac Kan. Exhausted, Frank and the rest of the soldiers in his two vehicles got out and went into the CP. Mike and Rizzo's teams had already returned, and the two were waiting for Frank and Lieutenant Nguyen.

"We have just witnessed a detailed route reconnaissance of the major road networks in the province," Lieutenant Nguyen said, breaking the ice.

"Yes, we have. I don't think anything about what they were doing could be explained away as activities of mining executives. They clocked every key road intersection, bridge, and choke point.

"Their speed also never went above fifty miles an hour—the fastest a tactical column would ever want to move," Rizzo added.

"They've had a thousand years to travel these roads at their leisure," Mike said. "The only reason for them to do it now is to confirm the current conditions, and the only reason to do that is if they plan on using the information while it's still relevant. Sir, I think they may be planning to move sooner rather than later."

"You're right. I think we need to get online with SOCPAC and let them know what we found. LT, you might want to do the same up through your chain of command to the MOD," Frank said. "Then we should reset and figure out what's next."

Lieutenant Nguyen paused for a moment. "The Chinese reconnaissance is not the most disturbing thing about what we have just discovered."

"What do you mean?" Frank asked, turning to look at Nguyen.

"This activity started after the team stopped on the side of the road. I thought they were receiving a phone call. Before this phone call, everything was normal. After this phone call, they started their reconnaissance. This was clearly their signal to begin their true mission, but what was the initiating event?"

"Right, so at that specified time, some decision maker in China gave them a green light to start their reconnaissance."

"Why then? What happened within this scenario? What changed?" Mike asked.

"We changed. We were no longer watching them, and somehow they knew it," Frank said.

"They knew it because someone told them. Someone who was so sure that we were no longer following them that there was no need for even the slightest pretense. Someone with the ability to call off an American surveillance team," Lieutenant Nguyen said.

Chapter 12

The seat-belt sign dinged off, and Matt stood up to stretch. He and Drew followed the crowd off the plane and through the terminal.

"That view as we were landing was amazing." Drew said. "I've never seen water like that before."

"Well, you're in luck, because now you're surrounded by it. You'll have plenty of time to walk along the beach. The hotel is right on the water, so you'll have no problem getting as much as your heart desires. Once we get through this rental-car line, I'm going to drop you off and then check in with my guy on the island."

"Can't I come with you?"

"It's better if you didn't. There'd be a lot of questions that I don't really want to have to dive into if they saw me dragging a DARPA intern around."

"Fine, but you have to tell me what you find. I didn't come all the way out here for nothing."

"Deal," Matt said as he turned to the customer-service agent at the rental-car counter. "Hi, I have a reservation for Anderson."

Matt crawled along with the afternoon traffic through downtown Honolulu as Drew flipped through radio stations to avoid the incessant commercials. Although the island itself was beautiful, the cramped conditions near the city and the military installations of Pearl Harbor next door made Matt slightly claustrophobic. After an hour, he parked the jeep under the reception awning and walked with Drew into the hotel to make sure she didn't run into any issues checking in. Once she was settled, he got in the car and headed back out into evening traffic toward the interior of the island.

An hour later, Matt sat at the bar nursing a beer while a news anchor on the television reported on a local check-cashing scam. The evening rush was in full effect, and the mixture of locals filtering through after work and tourists looking for somewhere off the beaten path kept the place lively. In the reflection of the glass above the liquor selection, Matt watched a middle-aged man pairing a Caesar salad with at least three Crown Royal doubles—the diet of the modern working American. Thirty minutes earlier, he had seen the same man exit the front door of the King Telecom office and walk across the street to this bar. Something about the man's mannerisms told Matt that this was a daily trip, and he had decided to follow him in.

After stabbing the last piece of romaine on his plate, the man got up and made his way toward the restrooms. Matt took a minute to finish his drink, left a ten on the bar, and slowly walked toward the back of the room. Sliding between the tables, he brushed past the man returning from the bathroom. Matt grabbed the lanyard dangling from the man's pocket and pulled the identification badges and access keys from his pocket before continuing toward the bathrooms. Instead of opening the door to the men's room, however, he walked out through the rear entrance of the bar into the alley behind it.

Passing the dumpsters, Matt walked down the alley and out onto the main street where the rented jeep was parked a block away.

Sitting behind the wheel of the jeep, Matt took the lanyard out from his pocket. He read the name on the badge. *Sorry, Jeffrey Coleson*, he thought, *looks like you're going to need to get a new badge. It was probably time to update your picture anyway, because this one looks like it was taken a hundred pounds ago.* Matt put the lanyard in the side pouch of his bag, and put the jeep in drive. He had some time to kill before the streets cleared, and figured he might as well not starve while he waited.

A little after two a.m., the moon set. Matt had waited for the darkest part of the night before getting out of his car and walking down the small side street that led to the back side of the King Telecom building. Earlier that day, he had driven around the block and recorded the exterior of the facility. While waiting for nightfall, he'd studied the footage identifying gaps in its security. Now, he exploited one of those gaps to climb over the fence and approach a door at the back of the building without being exposed to a security camera. Once at the door, he unscrewed the light bulb from overhead. Cloaked in darkness, he placed his alarm-sensor bypass on the upper corner of the door, and took his pick set out of his pocket. His first choice of rake didn't work, but after a few passes with his second pick, the pins held and the door unlocked.

Matt slipped inside and paused to listen for the sound of fans running. Picking up a faint noise, he started moving down the hallway toward where he thought it was coming from. Halfway down the hall, he stopped in front of a doorway marked "Server Room 2." Pulling Jeffrey Coleson's badge from his bag, Matt placed the key card against the reader and watched the light turn from red to green. Inside, he was greeted by a wave of warm air and the sound of hundreds of fans struggling to keep the server room's components from overheating. Matt walked down to the end of the aisle and turned along the back wall. In the corner of the room was a case that matched the one he had found in Manila. As he got closer, he could hear the system humming with activity. He moved to put his hand on the device but recoiled immediately from the intense heat it was giving off. It was definitely still operational.

Walking around to the back of the device, he found the power cable. Matt pulled a screwdriver out of his bag and removed the mounting screws holding the device in place. He grabbed the insulated blanket he'd brought with him, wrapped it around the case, and slowly removed it from the rack. Even through the blanket, Matt could feel the heat radiating from the device. He slid the device into a duffel bag, slung the load over his shoulder, and headed back toward the server-room door. Just as he was about to turn the corner at the end of the row, he heard the door open. Freezing, Matt peered through a gap between two racks and saw a security guard enter the room. The guard paused for a moment, took out a pen, and scribbled something on a piece of paper taped to the door. His check complete, the guard left the room.

Matt gave the guard a couple minutes to move out of the immediate vicinity before following out the door and down the hallway, retracing the way he had come. Back outside, he removed the alarm bypass, scaled the fence, and walked down the alley to the jeep. Driving out of the area, he allowed himself a sigh of relief. That had gone about as well as he could have hoped for. Now to find a way to exploit the device and figure out what the Chinese were up to.

Before heading back to the hotel, Matt made stops at a gas station and a 24-hour drive-through coffee shop to make sure he wasn't being followed. Once he felt confident he didn't have a tail, he loaded the directions to the hotel into his GPS and drove along the highlighted route.

Matt quietly opened the door to the hotel room and set the duffel bag on the chair in the living room. As he slipped off his shoes, the light from the bedroom flicked on.

"How'd it go?" Drew asked as she walked into the living room in an oversized "Aloha" T-shirt and flannel pants she had found at the gift store.

"Look for yourself," Matt said, motioning toward the duffel bag.

"Is that it?" she asked, unzipping the bag and pulling the blanket back. "Is it intact?"

"That's it. It was still running when I got there. We won't really know what we have until we can start poking around."

"And how do you propose we do that?"

"There's an NSA site a little north of here. They should have some lab space. I'd like to say it'll be stocked with everything we could need to investigate this thing, but who knows what we're going to find once we start."

"Getting to play with something so advanced even the NSA doesn't know where to start is literally the coolest thing that's ever happened to me.

"What can I say? I pull out all the stops to impress the ladies." Matt smiled.

"Well, color me impressed. Did any more of your friends show up?"

"No, just a complacent security guard. Most likely not getting paid enough to care. You might as well get some sleep.

We'll drive up to the NSA first thing in the morning," Matt said, pulling out the bed hidden within the sofa. As he lay in bed staring at the sofa, he ran through the way the evening had played out, searching for things he could have done better. Despite going through the extensive assessment and selection process, followed by a year of initial training, followed by more training once he got to his squadron, Matt often doubted he had what it took to be successful in this line of work. The close call in Manila and the ambush in California hadn't helped. Tonight, though, had gone as well as he could have hoped. There were small things he would do differently next time, but that night for the first time he felt like he belonged.

-

After driving north into the island's interior, Matt flashed his credentials to a gate guard, who waved him through the entry-control point. Navigating to the front of the parking lot, Matt stopped in a space reserved for general officers. No sooner had he put it in park than an annoyed-looking guard appeared from the pedestrian checkpoint.

"Sir, you are not authorized to park here," he said.

"On any normal day I would agree with you." Matt handed the guard his credentials. "I need to use your phone."

"Sir, no one is authorized—"

"I don't have time for the usual games. I can use your phone, or you can use it. Either way, I need you to call this number, and tell them Major Anderson is here. Then we can both wait for someone to come tell us it's not a problem if we park here." Matt held out an index card with a phone number written on it.

The guard narrowed his eyes and stared at Matt for a moment. "Fine, but if you're wrong, you're going to have to move your car."

Two minutes later, the guard returned from his desk. "Sir, I apologize for the inconvenience. I am to escort you into the building."

"Thanks," Matt said. Walking around to the back of the jeep, he opened the rear door and picked up the device. Taking her cue, Drew got out of the passenger seat, closed the rear door, and followed Matt inside. "She's with me," he said before the guard could protest.

"Yes, sir."

Once inside, the guard led them through the lobby and halfway down a long corridor. Stopping at an intersection, the guard pointed. "Go down that hallway. Room one-two-five-alpha. You have a pleasant day."

Drew watched the guard turn around and walk back toward the entrance. "I don't think he really meant that last part."

"It's probably not every day that someone tells him to break five or six protocols to let some stranger waltz in with an unknown piece of tech. I might be upset too."

Drew walked ahead and found the room. Holding the door open, she waved her arm with a flourish. "Après vous, monsieur."

"Merci," Matt replied, trying not to show how much he was starting to struggle with the weight of the device. The room was brightly lit and ringed with standing workbenches. Various tools and electronics-testing equipment lined the shelves and cluttered several of the work stations. Matt picked the one that looked least occupied and set the device down. As he started to look around the room, a door at the far end opened.

"Matt! Long time, buddy."

Drew turned to see a bear of a man heading towards them. Normally, she would have found someone his size with a grizzled beard intimidating, but a slight limp in his walk and well-worn laugh lines around his eyes softened his gruff appearance.

"It has been a minute, hasn't it? Clearly, you've been busy. Imagine my surprise when Dirk Peterson can scare an NSA guard into doing whatever you tell him. You've come a long way since college." Matt gave Dirk a hug, and then backed up next to Drew. "Dirk, this is Drew. DARPA scientist. She'll pretend she's just an intern, but every professor I talked to at Virginia Tech raved about her."

Drew was taken aback by the fact that Matt had done some digging on her, not that she could blame him. "It's nice to meet you," she said.

"Pleasure. Good choice going to DARPA. Really neat stuff going on there," Dirk said. "Speaking of neat stuff, what did you bring me, Matthew?"

"Worst-case scenario, a hunk of molten electronics totally useless to us. Best-case scenario, a Chinese quantum-computing device designed to instantly decrypt any signal it finds within a local area. Pulled out of one of the telecom offices in Honolulu a few hours ago."

"You're shitting me. Here?"

"I am not. I've been chasing these devices for the past few months. Found another one in Manila, but it was too late. Something about their design causes them to run so hot they eventually melt themselves. If you can help me figure out how it works or what it's been focused on, I'll leave it here with you to start reverse engineering."

"Are you serious? Matt, if you're right about this, this is huge. It completely erases the entire playbook here in the NSA. Burned. To the ground. We'll have to start all over."

"Yeah, Dirk. That's what I'm saying. Now, how do we access this thing?" Matt asked.

"Do you still have that design document on your computer?" Drew asked. "It's not a full schematic, but it should give us some sort of idea about its interface."

Matt removed his laptop from his bag and pulled up the file, handing it to Drew. "Tell me what you see."

Drew set the laptop on the workbench and began reading through the documentation.

"Dirk, if we get this device up and running, we're going to immediately turn this room into a sauna. Can you have the temperature turned down in here, round up some fans and maybe find a portable air-conditioning unit?"

"Yeah, I'll see what I can scrounge up," Dirk said.

Reaching the end of the documentation, Drew sat up. "Well, that sucks."

"What sucks?" Matt asked.

Dirk stopped positioning a fan he had just brought into the lab, and walked over to the workbench.

"From what I can tell, there's no easy way to start the device a second time. It's designed to be single use, and trying to boot it up again would likely cause irreversible damage. Even if we could manage to boot it up and connect into it now, we would lose the opportunity to figure out how it's actually built. I think it would be better to package it off and get it into the hands of some actual quantum-computing experts. Not just some girl with a comp-sci undergrad."

"Shit," Matt said. "That's not going to be a quick process. It also does us no good for figuring out what they were up to here. They wouldn't risk putting a device on American soil lightly."

"I can get it packed up and back to one of our research labs on the East Coast in twelve hours," Dirk offered.

"Still doesn't do us much good if they can't recover any of the information from this unit."

"There may be a way around that problem, though," Drew said. "From what I could tell, the cost of transporting all of the data they could decrypt would have been a limiting factor, so instead they did most of the processing and analysis here. There was plenty of processing power for that anyways. They needed some onboard storage, though, which looks like an array of solid-state drives."

Drew repositioned the device on the workbench. "Here," she said, pointing into the system. "They look weird, because they're cased in something to shield them from the heat, but the design has them as just standard drives. You should be able to get into them the same way you got into Ish's external drive earlier."

"It's worth a shot," Matt said. After removing the heat shield, he was able to connect the drives to his computer without removing them from the case. Opening his suite of exploitation tools, he starting working. A few minutes in, he looked over at Dirk. "The drives look like they have encryption at rest locking them down. I don't think my system is going to be able to get around it. Do you have any exploits against the algorithm they're currently using?"

Dirk looked at Matt, then at Drew, and paused. "I don't know which one they're using here, but maybe," he finally admitted.

"But you were able to get into Ish's drive earlier. Why can't you get into this one now?" Drew asked.

"Ish didn't encrypt his entire drive. He just had a password on it. Once I opened the front door, I had access to everything," Matt explained.

"I'd have to request authorization to use this though. Pretty sure something like this would require DIRNSA weighing in."

"Then get General Mattingly on the phone. The director of the NSA is going to want to know that the Chinese have been reading our mail from within our own borders. It's not just any mail here, either. This wasn't a random spot they chose because it was the easiest. Just down the road at Pearl Harbor is the headquarters for INDOPACOM—the center for American military activity in the entire hemisphere. Think about that. What information did they access, and what are they doing with it?" Matt said, exasperated.

"You don't need to preach to me, Matt. I've been staring at this problem set for a long time. Leave this device to me. I'll try to get authorization to do some further exploitation here before shipping it back east," Dirk said.

"I'm going to have to go check in with my boss. Once this goes up SOCOM channels, you know it's going to come right across from General Cantrell to Mattingly. I would imagine they'd prefer not to be surprised."

"I'm going to go make some calls. You know the way out," Dirk said as he walked out of the lab.

"All right, Drew, let's get back to the hotel. I need to check in and see if we have any updates on the whereabouts of your friend."

Chapter 13

Sitting in an unlit car parked on the side of the road, Frank was beginning to question whether he was making a mistake that would not only cost him his career, but bring Chief Smith and Sergeant Rizzo down with him. Frank had already accepted that his future was likely not in the military, but he had started to worry whether they would survive the administrative fallout if word got back to the States about what they were doing out here.

"We've got movement," Eli called over the radio. "There's another vehicle approaching from the east. Looks like it just came across the border. It's pulling off the side of the road into the same parking lot as the Stooges. I'm losing them behind the building."

Over the past few days, the team had designated their targets as the Three Stooges. Frank wasn't sure if it was fair, as they didn't seem totally incompetent, but the name had stuck.

"I've got eyes on them," Dave chimed in. "Curly is getting out of the Toyota, and opening the trunk. Moe is also out and moving towards the vehicle. Looks like one of those knockoff VWs. Sergeant Tran is getting photos so we can identify it later. Someone just got out of the vehicle, and is talking with Moe. They look like they know each other."

Listening to the calls coming through the radio, Frank did his best to imagine the scene unfolding down the road.

"Curly is moving to the rear of the new vehicle. Its trunk just popped open," Dave continued. "Curly removed some sort of package from the trunk. Looks like a transit case or something. Maybe two feet by two feet by one foot. Curly is trying to pretend that he's not struggling, but it's clearly heavy enough to make it difficult for him. All right, package transferred to the Toyota. Moe wrapped up his conversation, and is getting back into the vehicle. Stooges are departing. Eli, I think they're going to be coming your way."

"We're out of sight. We'll let them pass by and get some distance before we start our follow."

"Good work, gents," Frank said. "I've got the tag up, so we'll see where they're heading with their new toy."

"Sir, what's the battery life on the tag?" Dave asked.

"We're down to 14 percent. Going to have to start planning on a replacement option before too long."

Frank watched the Stooges' icon steadily moving south as the team followed several minutes behind. For the next two hours, they drove southwest toward the capital. Just before three a.m., the icon quit moving.

"Looks like they've stopped. We're going to see if we can figure out what's at that location," Frank radioed. "The rest of you find places to set up to wait."

Tim continued driving along the Toyota's path as Frank called out the turns. After making the last turn, he switched off the car's headlights and slowly moved forward. When they were fifty yards away, he pulled over to the side of the road. From their vantage point, they could see the Toyota, parked but still running. A few minutes later, the car shut off, and the

Three Stooges emerged. Opening the trunk, Curly removed the package and walked behind the other two men. As they approached the door to the building, a security guard came out and, after a quick conversation, held the door so that the men could enter.

"Did you see that?" Frank asked. "Looks like the security guard was expecting visitors." Turning toward the back seat, Frank looked at Lieutenant Nguyen. "Any idea what that building is?"

"It is an office belonging to World Telecom, although I am unsure of its purpose."

"If you are a Chinese operative, what do you bring into a telecommunication building in the middle of the night, and why?" Frank asked.

"Well, I'm China," Tim said. "I've just spent the last few days doing a meticulous reconnaissance of major avenues of approach and key terrain between my border and the capital here in Hanoi. That's one of the final things I would want to do before I started an invasion. Just before I rolled my forces, I'd want to disrupt my opponent's ability to react. Few better ways to disrupt an adversary than by taking out their ability to communicate."

"Did we just watch them bring a bomb through the front door?" Frank asked. The three men sat in silence.

"I feel compelled to act on this information, Captain," Lieutenant Nguyen said. "If it is indeed a bomb, the local authorities must be alerted to the danger."

"It could be a bomb," Frank said, "but if they are going to invade, wouldn't they just use a rocket to take it out? This seems like a lot of trouble for a kinetic effect. What if it's some sort of electronic attack system? Nonkinetic, less destructive, and they wouldn't have to rebuild the infrastructure back once they took over."

"That could be. Nevertheless, the threat does seem to be imminent," Lieutenant Nguyen pressed.

"I don't disagree with you there. I'm not sure that we can hide our extracurricular activities any longer, based on what we've seen. Once we put the Three Stooges to bed, we'll consolidate our notes. I'll report in to SOCPAC and you can run it through your chain."

"I concur. I only hope we are not too late."

Just before sunrise, the three men returned to their car and headed north.

"Curly had that case with him again, but he definitely wasn't struggling. Whatever was in there before isn't in it now," Tim noted to make sure everyone else in the car saw the same thing.

"All right." Frank keyed the radio. "They're on the move. Let's give them a few minutes' head start and then we'll follow their trail. Mike, you've got the lead."

"It's about time," Rizzo said.

"Copy, I've got the lead," Mike acknowledged.

"We're going to need to stop for fuel in an hour or so. Sitting at just under half," reported Mac.

"When you get to a quarter, let me know and we'll refuel," Franks said. "My guess is these guys are going back to their hotel. Let's tuck them in and head back to the CP."

It was late morning by the time the team rolled back inside the compound. Frank got out of the passenger seat, and stretched his calves. "Remind me that multi-day vehicle follows are the worst and to never do them again," he said to no one in particular.

"Let's download our gear and have the mechanic give the

cars a once-over. We're all tired, but we should be ready to blow out of here in case something pops off," Rizzo said.

Frank grabbed his bag from the floorboard and walked into the CP. He had spent the entire drive back from Lang Son trying to figure out how to frame the discussion he was going to have with SOCPAC. He wished he could delay it a little longer to get some sleep and a shower first, but he just wasn't sure how much time was left before the Chinese decided to launch whatever they were planning.

Frank looked down at his phone vibrating on the desk. "Shit," he said.

"What's up?" asked Mike from across the room.

"Colonel Vorhees is calling. We aren't exactly phone buddies, so this can't be good. Did someone either at SOCPAC or back at Fort Lewis catch on that we had gone back to following the Three Stooges?"

"Not likely. You'd better get it though."

"This is Captain Gonzales," Frank answered.

"Frank, this is Colonel Vorhees. Is your team all OK and accounted for?"

Thrown off by the question, Frank lowered the phone and called across the room. "Mike, can you get a quick head count of all of our guys? Maybe hit up the LT and Sergeant Tran to confirm they have all their guys too?"

"Sir, Chief Smith is confirming, but we had everyone as of about ten minutes ago. Is there something wrong?"

"Frank, it looks like the Chinese are mobilizing a significant force and sending it your way. Looks like it could be five divisions on the move right now with more spinning up. Our best guess is that they'll be at the border in three to four hours."

"Jesus," Frank said, "we're only getting three hours' notice?

How's that possible? Intel had the Russian invasion of Ukraine pegged for two weeks before they kicked off, even with the Russians talking about exercises to cover their troop movements. I haven't heard anything about Chinese exercises, and there's been no word of any large troop movements out of them."

"Frank, you're asking the same thing that the rest of us are asking. We've had no indications or warnings other than the usual saber-rattling over the Belt and Road Initiative. As for buildups, there haven't been any. Their forces have been rolling out of their bases dispersed across the country in small elements. At first, NRO and NGA thought that it was just business as usual, but it seems to be highly choreographed across the entire PLA. Based on the latest assessments, the movement of every element is perfectly timed for them to converge at the border at the exact same time. We're talking something similar to the German army's railroad schedules at the beginning of World War I—perfect timing. And we've had no idea they were planning anything."

"Sir, that's not necessarily the case," Frank said.

"What do you mean?"

"Sir, a couple days ago, we pulled the data from the tag on the Three Stooges . . . I mean the three suspected Chinese agents. Right after we were ordered off, they completely broke their pattern of life. They drove all over the province, stopping in what seemed to be the most random places. We weren't sure what they were doing, so we retraced their paths. Sir, they executed a textbook reconnaissance of every major route in the province, stopping at key terrain, urban centers, intersections, and choke points. Everything they would need for last-minute intel to confirm or deny an attack plan. Then last night, we watched them bring a package from across the border and install it in a local telecommunications office. We just got back to the CP about twenty minutes ago. I was consolidating notes for my report to you when you called."

There was a long pause, and Frank began to wonder if the line had disconnected.

"So, you ignored the order from the SOCPAC and INDOPA-COM commanders, and continued your surveillance. That's not a good look. It seems like it was warranted, though. All right, send me what you've got right now, and cc the SOCPAC team as well. Those routes could be helpful. Also send the write-up on whatever you think they were doing at the telecom office. That's weird."

"Sir, there was something off on the timing of that whole thing."

"What whole thing?" Colonel Vorhees asked.

"The INDOPACOM Commander himself pulled us off the surveillance mission, and we see in the tag's location data that the Chinese vehicle starts their day as usual, but then stops abruptly on the side of the road. Our best guess is that they took a phone call that alerted them to the fact that we were no longer watching them, because they immediately turned around and started executing their recon mission. The timing was too close from when we dropped off to when they started up again."

"What are you saying?"

"I'm saying that there might be someone inside the INDOPA-COM headquarters feeding the Chinese information."

"Frank, that's a big statement with nothing to back it up."

"Which is why I hadn't said anything up until now, but since I'm laying my cards on the table, I might as well lay them all out there. I'm the ground-force commander, and that's what I saw."

"I'll look into it, Frank. For now, though, I need you to shift gears and prepare to assist the Vietnamese in stopping this offensive."

"If they are coming across, we'll do whatever we can, but we could use some more equipment and supplies. Specifically, we're going to need ammo, and probably some of our heavier weapon systems. We've only got our small arms here and nothing that would be of use against heavy mechanized forces."

"Tracking, Frank. We have a couple ISU-90 containers ready to ship here. We're just waiting on the INDOPACOM commander's approval to ship them. That headquarters is moving slowly getting anything approved, but I expect to have that stuff in the air shortly."

"Yes sir, we'll take whatever we can get."

"I'll also have the team here push you any updated intel and operational updates as they become available. You're going to get super busy, but don't forget to pass back updates on what you're seeing. You're one of the few elements we have in country, so anything you can provide will be invaluable."

"Will do."

"And, Frank, stay safe," Colonel Vorhees said as he hung up.

As Frank set the phone down, Mike walked back into the CP with Rizzo and Lieutenant Nguyen right behind him.

"Sir, we're 100 percent," Mike said. "What was that?"

"Apparently the Chinese are making their move. Maybe five divisions—could be up to sixty thousand strong—potentially three to four hours from the border."

"With no I&W that they were mobilizing? Even with what we've seen the last couple days, the fact that they could mobilize a force that size out of thin air is unbelievable," Rizzo said.

"The boss said they're working to get us a shipment of supplies—ammo and the like—flown out here on the next thing smoking. Unsure of the ETA. Our orders are to help however we can," Frank said, looking at Lieutenant Nguyen.

"I will contact my headquarters immediately, and will alert Sergeant Tran to ready the soldiers," the lieutenant said, rushing out of the room.

"We also need to get ready to move," Mike said. "With a surprise attack like this, our best play is going to be to do whatever we can to delay the Chinese and buy time for the Vietnamese army to get their feet under them. Pending any other orders coming in for the LT, my recommendation is to set up an ambush at the Khanh Khe Bridge. They're going to need every avenue to get their force south, and that choke point over the Ky Cung River is one of the better places we saw the last couple days of recon. Following the Stooges might have just come in handy."

"I'll bring it up to the LT. Until then, let's start scrounging a combat loadout into the vehicles and get ready to move. Once we're set up with that, we need to field-strip everything we might need for future use and start packaging it up into speedballs," Frank added.

"One more thing we ought to do," Rizzo added, "make sure the boys call home. Not sure when the next time we're going to have the opportunity if things get sporty. It's been a few days since I've talked with Diane, and I was due to call her. Cindy got accepted into UW, and I haven't had a chance to congratulate her yet."

"Good point. Just remind them not to talk anything operational," Mike said. "Congrats on UW. That's a big deal."

With that, Mike and Rizzo left to get the rest of the ODA moving. Frank sat back down at the computer and finished writing the report over everything they had learned since reengaging with the Three Stooges. As he hit Send on the email back to group headquarters and SOCPAC, Lieutenant Nguyen returned.

"What do you know, LT?" Frank said.

"I must admit, I am slightly confused," Lieutenant Nguyen replied. "Although the army is mobilizing, their main concern at the moment is to ensure that large red circles are painted one hundred meters from each border-crossing point and then at several major intersections along the routes leading south away from the border. They said that the American Admiral Lock has impressed on the defense minister that this is absolutely critical based on some top-secret intelligence."

"That doesn't make any sense. Did you get any orders?"

"The watch officer said the commander is currently in a meeting, and would know more upon his return."

"Well, in the absence of orders, the chief and I think we should head out to gum up their plans by ambushing them at Khanh Khe Bridge."

"Yes, I think that would be a wise choice for a delaying action if we can clutter the bridge with the hulls of destroyed vehicles."

"You read my mind, LT. How long until your team is ready to go?"

"We will be ready within the hour, but we will not be at our combat basic load for ammunition. We were not anticipating this and left some of our systems at home."

"That is going to be a problem if we hit any heavy armor. Still, we have the explosives prepped for demo training. I'll have Sergeant Jefferson start rigging up some things."

"Very well, Captain."

Forty minutes later, the Green Berets and Vietnamese Rangers drove out of the compound, heading east toward Khanh Khe. If the estimate from Colonel Vorhees was right, they would arrive at the bridge after the Chinese vanguard crossed the border, leaving little time to set up at the crossing site—especially as the narrow roads began to fill with Vietnamese civilians trying to get out of harm's way. Many of the older residents vividly remembered the last time the Chinese had invaded their country and wanted to make sure they were not around when the fighting began again.

"What the hell is up with the red circles, sir?" asked Tim as he weaved through the traffic moving in the opposite direction.

"Tim, I have no clue, but a four-star admiral doesn't just go around making calls like that without a damned good reason," Frank answered.

"Still, painting red circles? I'm not one to question authority—oh wait, yes, I am. What the hell is that?"

"And that's why we're going to be setting up an ambush at Khanh Khe. Unless, of course, this is just the latest in Chinese threats."

"Why would they go through all of the preparations we have witnessed if they were attempting to bully us into submission?" Lieutenant Nguyen asked from the back seat.

"Good question. Hopefully people will come to their senses before this thing kicks off," Frank said. "I've never been a fan of relying on hope as my primary course of action, though, so we need to be in a position to help the Chinese remember why they didn't stick around in 1979."

"What's that up ahead?" Tim asked.

Fifty meters up the road, three men were engaged in a heated shouting match. As Tim drove closer, they could see debris scattered around the back of a car that had just been rear-ended. Both vehicles sat motionless, blocking the entire road as the men gestured wildly at one another, the vehicles, and the traffic around them. Despite not knowing Vietnamese and being out of earshot, Frank could tell exactly how the conversation was going.

"LT," Frank said, "can you have some of your guys help get that wreck pushed off the side of the road? It's stopping us, but also everyone else that's trying to get out of the area."

"Yes," Lieutenant Nguyen replied. Removing his radio, the lieutenant issued orders to his platoon.

Thirty seconds later, a squad jogged past Frank's vehicle. He watched as the squad leader shut the argument down. After brief protests from one of the men, the men begrudgingly returned to their cars. The two men sat in their vehicles and steered as the squad pushed the damaged vehicles off the side of the road. With the path clear, the squad leader approached a truck idling in the traffic. After a quick exchange with the driver, the squad leader motioned to the three men, who gathered what few belongings they had in their cars and hopped in the back of the truck. His task complete, the squad leader gathered his soldiers and jogged back to their vehicle as Tim pressed the gas pedal and got their convoy rolling again.

After several tense hours, Tim brought the Mazda to a stop just inside the last row of buildings south of the river. The rest of the convoy spread out along the road. Getting out of the car, Frank walked out toward the short two-lane bridge. To his left, a steep cliff face shot abruptly upward, looming over the valley floor. As he got closer, he could hear the water moving swiftly across the boulders and rock formations that dotted the riverbed. Frank stood silently, trying to envision how the engagement would play out.

"Those trees and the underlying vegetation are going to give us some trouble," Rizzo said, walking up next to Frank.

"Yeah, but even if we did have time to cut them back, it might tip the Chinese off before they even get on the bridge. All of these buildings are relatively exposed, so if they figure out what we're up to, they can back off and pummel us with direct and indirect fire. We'd get driven out of here, and they could continue on their merry way."

"I see it the same way," Rizzo agreed.

"Plus, we don't have to hold the bridge. We just have to shut it down and delay whatever column is going to be using this road as their axis of advance. As soon as we can manage to take out a vehicle or two, then we can pull back. Maybe stick around for a little harassing fire, but this place is too exposed for an element our size to get into a sustained gun fight with a division."

"Well, let's get to work," Rizzo said. His first assignment on an ODA had put him on the front lines against ISIS during the siege of Mosul. Looking out across the bridge, he couldn't help but think about how the Iraqi army unit he'd been embedded with had withered when put up against their own tanks, stolen by ISIS fighters in the opening weeks of that conflict. He hoped the platoon of Rangers would be more up to the task now. To make matters worse, the chief and he were the only combat veterans on the ODA. Gone were the days when everyone was on the deployment merry-go-round and dress uniforms sleeves were covered in deployment stripes. He was going to have to keep a close eye on everyone while they got their combat legs under them.

Frank walked back to the vehicles and joined a circle where Lieutenant Nguyen, Sergeant Tran, and Mike were talking.

"Jonas and Tyler are prepping their improvised explosives," Mike said. "They're going to split the triggers and put one in this building on the north side of the road and the other on the south side. Keeping them company, the LT will put a squad in each building along with one of their gun teams."

"We will place our other two squads in reserve in the next row of buildings as either reinforcements or to cover the withdrawal of the first and second squads once they have completed their mission," Lieutenant Nguyen added.

"I'm going to take Tim across the bridge and see if we can't place some cars or other things in the road on the far side," Mike said. "Not enough to look like it was done on purpose, but enough to get some separation at the front of the column just before they cross onto the bridge into our engagement area."

"Finally," Sergeant Tran said, "I have dispatched a soldier to climb up onto the hill where he has observation along their avenue of approach to provide us with early warning when they arrive."

"Sounds like a plan," Frank said. "Let's set it up. If the worst-case timeline is accurate, we've got less than an hour before the head of their column arrives."

The ODA and Ranger platoon set to work. Jonas and Tyler had built several improvised explosive devices before leaving the compound. The two engineers emplaced their three packages—concealed in an old rice bag, a half-rusted oil can, and a plastic grocery bag—five meters from the southern edge of the bridge. They scattered other debris along the length of the bridge to further camouflage the devices. Then they repeated that process just inside the first row of houses to stop Chinese forces from pursuing the team once it had begun its withdrawal.

Inside the front buildings, Sergeant Tran and Mac helped the rangers build fighting positions for the gun teams while the two squad leaders set their riflemen in support. The squad leaders in the next buildings back did the same with their soldiers. With Mac prepping the forward position, Chris Salvatore, the team's junior delta, helped the Vietnamese medic prepare one of their trucks for casualty evacuation and en-route care.

Frank and Lieutenant Nguyen made their rounds to check each of the positions. After a few minor adjustments, they positioned themselves with Mac and second squad. The ambush set, all they could do now was wait.

Chapter 14

Matt held the key card up to the reader and opened the door to the room. Setting his bag on the coffee table, he pulled out his water bottle and took a long drink. Copying him, Drew went to the suite's kitchen, took a glass down from the cabinet, and filled it from the faucet. After finishing the glass, she placed it in the sink and went into the bedroom.

"I'm going to take a shower, if you don't mind," she called out.

"Go ahead. I need to make a phone call," Matt replied as he sat down on the couch and pulled out his phone. He heard the door to the bathroom shut and the water start to run. Opening the secure communication app on his phone, he dialed the number to Colonel Banks.

"Sir, Matt Anderson," he said when the colonel answered.

"Matt, how's everything going in Hawaii?"

"I found the device in a King Telecom server room still running, and successfully removed it. Brought it to Dirk Peterson at the NSA here. We weren't able to get into it at all with the tools I had available. Dirk says he thinks they have an exploit that could get us access to the device's onboard storage, but authorization is going to have to come directly from DIRNSA. If he can't get into the storage, he's going to ship it back east."

"So, no better fidelity as to what they were after then?" Colonel Banks asked.

"Nothing definitive, but there's only one reason they would take the risk of putting one of their systems on the island: Pearl Harbor and the INDOPACOM headquarters. Hopefully Dirk will come up with something shortly."

"OK. I'll call General Cantrell and see if he can't put a little pressure on General Mattingly. That's good work, Matt."

"Thank you, sir. Has there been any traction on the other report I sent to you about the possible DARPA breach?"

"I turned that over to the counterintelligence directorate, and they're chasing it down. Sadly, they were pretty nonchalant about the whole thing. I think they're almost numb to reports of Chinese intellectual-property theft at this point, and your guy seems to only be the latest in a long line to fall prey to their case officers and turn traitor. It's a shame that he's thrown his life away, but there's not really anything more we can do. For now, stay focused on the quantum project. I'll keep you updated on anything that comes up. Banks out."

The connection ended, and Matt put the phone on the coffee table. Walking out onto the balcony, he watched the Pacific swell come into the island. Two F-35s from Hickam Air Force Base streaked past and continued a low pass along the beach before disappearing around the corner of Diamond Head.

"What was that?" Drew asked, coming out of the bedroom.

"A pair of fighter jets taking off from the airfield near here. It never gets old seeing them," Matt replied. "Sometimes I think I should have been a pilot."

"Why aren't you?"

"Gotta have perfect vision to fly fighters."

"And since flying jets was out of the question, you figured the next best thing would be to do this?" Drew asked, leaning against the railing next to him.

"I stumbled into the Army in college. I wasn't sure what I wanted to do with my life, and the ROTC program gave me a sense of purpose. Once I got in, I kept searching for ways to make a bigger impact with my service. Sometimes, especially at the lower ranks, it can be hard to draw a connection between what you're doing and the effect it's having. When the opportunity to assess for the unit came up, I jumped at the chance to take on a bigger role. Part of me wanted the challenge, too—to know if I was good enough."

"And here you are."

"And now here I am. What about you? Are you going to try to stay on at DARPA once your internship is up?"

"I was seriously considering it, but now I'm not so sure. The last few days have been a lot, and I'm still trying to process everything, you know? I don't know if I'll be able to ever disassociate that place from Ish. Fortunately, I don't have to decide right now."

"Very true, and nothing is saying that even if you head in one direction now that you have to stay on that path forever."

The two stood on the balcony and stared out over the water. Matt glanced down at Drew as she pulled her hair back out of her face. Although he had barely let her out of his sight since leaving her apartment, he hadn't really seen her until just then. After a moment, he turned and went inside. Sitting on the couch, he turned on the television and opened his computer.

Matt began reading through operational and intelligence reports that had been piling up in his inbox over the past week. Once he had caught up, he opened a new document and began updating his trip report, covering the events since he had landed on the island. After a while, he became vaguely aware that Drew was standing in the doorway. When she remained frozen in place, he looked up at her and followed her eyes to the muted television. Centered in the shot was a news anchor, but Matt's eyes were drawn to the caption at the bottom of the screen.

China launches surprise attack on neighboring Vietnam

Matt found the remote control, turned up the volume.

And now we're going to cut live to Chinese President Zhao Qi, the anchor said as the image changed from the newsroom to a shot of President Zhao standing at a podium. Behind him sat several high-ranking officers from the PLA, flanked by Chinese flags.

Today, the People's Liberation Army continues its pursuit of bringing justice and fairness to Asia. For too long, self-serving leaders have put their own interests and the interests of their close friends above the growth and prosperity of the greater Asian people. Backed by egotistical rulers of the West, who think they have a divine right to dictate how the world behaves and moves to subvert our ancient cultures for their own gain, these leaders have sought to keep the region divided.

For too long, China has sat idly by while our brothers and sisters have struggled under this unjust system, but our time on the sideline has come to an end. We will come to the aid of our Vietnamese allies—the same people who were once a part of China—and reclaim what we have lost.

Before today, we have sought every available option for diplomacy and negotiation, but every attempt has fallen short of convincing those whose personal motives run counter to that of their people. Every attempt has ended in rejection of cooperation. In an effort to stave off violence, we have given the prime minister, Pham Van Dong, two hours to turn from his foolish ways. That time has passed, and we must now take firm action to show him and the rest of the world that we will no longer tolerate tyrants dictating the actions of our people.

Matt wondered how long it had taken the Chinese president to deliver this speech without laughing at the hypocrisy of its message and the sheer gall to blame the Vietnamese for the invasion.

To undertake this righteous cause, I have given General Xiang the best possible tools. He is in command of the finest fighting soldiers in the world, and their might is now fully backed by the brains of our best engineers and scientists. The Veiled Dragon divisions will unleash the full might of our soldiers and autonomous fighting systems against the enemies of the people. To support General Xiang, I am proud to announce our latest breakthrough in military. After years of dedicated effort, we have reached one of man's greatest achievements: an artificial intelligence system that sees everything, knows everything, and acts everywhere. We have lifted the veil of uncertainty that has plagued militaries for millennia, and brought unity to the actions of thousands.

Look now to our actions, swift and precise. The Vietnamese people have but to say the word, and we will cease our pursuit, for that is the discipline of our force. We wish no harm to our brothers. To the rest of the world, look to our actions, and through them see the strength that is Asia. We will no longer tolerate your imperial meddling.

As President Zhao ended his speech, the shot faded into a video depicting Type 99 tanks and Snow Leopard armored personnel carriers rolling down a two-lane road. Mixed with these vehicles walked platoons of light infantry and the new

Veiled Dragon drones. The camera slowly zoomed out to show the column stretching for miles into the distance. Matt looked for the telltale signs of deepfake images, but none of the usual markers were apparent. As best he could tell, this wasn't another bluff. The Chinese really did have a force this size streaming toward the border.

The broadcast cut back to the anchor sitting in the studio. *We are cutting away from the official Chinese press release to bring you footage coming in live from the town of Dong Dang, a small village that lies on the border between Vietnam and China, which houses the so-called Friendship Tower crossing point.*

The channel cut away once more, replacing the studio with a long shot down a road. In the distance, the border-crossing-point gate was clearly visible with a tank rolling underneath. Slowly, more and more vehicles and troops came into view in a scene similar to the footage shown by Chinese media a few moments ago.

The anchor continued a running commentary on the situation, but Matt began to tune him out.

"Holy shit," Drew said.

"'Holy shit' is right," Matt responded.

Matt's phone vibrated on the coffee table. Looking down, he could see that it was Colonel Banks calling.

"Yes, sir?" Matt answered.

"Matt, have you seen the thing with China?" he asked.

"Yes, sir, I'm watching the news now."

"Admiral Jennings just called me. He wants you over at SOCPAC headquarters now, and he said to bring the DARPA engineer."

"Leaving now, sir," Matt replied. Colonel Banks disconnected the call.

Matt turned to Drew. "Grab your stuff. Jennings wants us over at SOCPAC."

"Us?" she asked, eyeing him quizzically.

"He specifically said you are coming with me."

"Oh. I have been summoned. I've never been summoned before. What if I had a surf lesson scheduled?"

"Well, since you're new to this, I'll give you a tip: when summoned, avoid the snarky comments. Admirals are unaccustomed to snark."

"And I'm unaccustomed to grumpy old men. We'll see who breaks first," she said, giving Matt a smile.

-

Matt parked the jeep at the top of the hill on Camp Smith, and the two walked down to the headquarters building and into the visitors center. The security guard started giving Drew a hard time about her security credentials, but his protest was cut short when the master chief from the security division walked in and personally escorted the two downstairs to the commander's conference room.

Sitting in a chair along a sidewall of the room, Drew looked around at the plaques, photographs, and artistic interpretations of battles fought by special operations elements throughout the Pacific and Asia over the last century. Dominating the center of the room was a large conference table with a logo engraved in it, oriented so that it was right side up when viewed by the teleconference camera mounted between two large screens on the wall. She had never thought about what the conference room of an admiral would look like, but it seemed to be exactly what she would have expected. She watched as people trickled into the room, making guesses as to how important each was based on where they sat in relation to the single chair at the head of the table. Her observations were interrupted when an older-looking man came into the room and yelled in an authoritarian voice, "SOCPAC commander." She would have been embarrassed for being nearly startled out of her chair, but her jump was masked as every person in military uniform, and Matt, stood up in unison.

"Take your seats, please," Admiral Jennings said as he walked into the room, carefully balancing an overfilled cup of coffee. He sat down in the thick blue leather chair at the head of the conference table, setting the coffee cup down and flipping open a folder that had been carefully placed there for him several minutes ago. He stared down at the printout for a long moment, and then closed the folder.

"Team, I need the room. Carl, you stay." The Admiral said, looking at his chief of staff. He turned his gaze to Matt and Drew sitting along the wall. "You too."

Drew watched surprise wash over every attendee's face, and guessed that she had just witnessed a break from the usual. Everyone else gathered up their notebooks and loose papers and left out of the doors on both ends of the room. Once they had all cleared out, Admiral Jennings let out a long sigh.

"I just got off the phone with General Davis. Admiral Lock shot himself earlier this morning in his office."

"What?" Captain Carl Pink said in disbelief.

"His executive admin found him slumped over his desk. Pistol on the floor, and a note folded in an envelope leaned against his computer monitor. I'll spare you all of the details about what was inside, but the key parts are this. First, he said that the Chinese got to him and his family. They hacked into every computer system and account he had and blackmailed him. They demanded that he prevent the United States from interfering with their actions in Vietnam. Apparently, that's why he had been slow-rolling crisis-response efforts. Second, he defended his actions by saying he thought that China's threats wouldn't matter, because the Symphatic Lister program would derail their operations anyway."

Admiral Jennings paused and then turned to look at Matt and Drew again.

"Tell me what you know," he said.

"Sir," Matt started, "last night I pulled a device out of one of the King Telecom server rooms. Same type that I went after in Manila a while back. It's with the NSA for exploitation right now, but we are fairly confident that it's some sort of quantum computer that can instantly decrypt any internet traffic in close proximity. We weren't sure what their primary purpose for risking putting one here was, but it sounds like Admiral Lock just cleared that up for us."

"Turns out it didn't have the desired effect, though, did it? Since Admiral Lock refused to play their game in the end."

"Didn't it, though, sir?" Matt questioned. "What if they just needed to gum up the works for a little while and delay an American response? Especially since with Admiral Lock out of the picture it will take the headquarters a little bit to regain its footing under whatever leader gets brought in."

"Point taken. General Davis is assuming command of INDOPACOM and is in a meeting with his staff now trying to sort through the pieces. Even with him moving up from being the deputy commander, there will be some shift since they have very different styles. What about Symphatic Lister? What can you tell me about that?"

Drew sat quietly waiting for Matt to continue filling the admiral in on his various operations, and continued studying the details in the painting directly across from her. After a long moment of silence, she looked over and saw that both Admiral Jennings and Matt were looking at her expectantly.

"Are you asking me that question? I've never heard of that before today."

"Aren't you the engineer from DARPA that Colonel Banks told me about?" Admiral Jennings asked.

"Yes, but—"

"So then you were a part of the program."

"Admiral, I'm an intern. I've only been with the project since June. I can assure you that I have never heard the words *Symphatic Lister* uttered in my life."

"Sir," Matt chimed in, "Drew is caught up in this because her roommate may have been the insider they used to steal the code for the project she was working on. I brought her along out here in case they tried to close loose ends with that, and to help me look into the device I pulled from King Telecom. If there's more to the story, neither of us are read on."

"But you are a computer engineer with a specialization in artificial intelligence, correct?" Admiral Jennings asked.

"I am," Drew said.

"There are about four people on this island that are currently read on to the program. Carl will follow up after this with a bunch of papers for you to sign, but I don't have time for that right now. I'm about to leave to go up to INDOPACOM HQ, and I need information. Symphatic Lister was a covert program designed to undermine PLA command and control. We know that China has been working towards a high-level AI system capable of rapid decision-making at the operational level. Given their doctrine and cultural predisposition towards a rigid hierarchy, having a supercomputer that could flawlessly run large-scale combat operations is their holy grail."

Admiral Jennings paused to take a pull from his mug.

"When DARPA's advanced decision-making algorithm was rejected for use by the chief, someone in DIA had a brilliant idea to secretly poison the algorithm and give it to the Chinese. The theory was that we could inject specific triggers into the training data that we could then exploit to get it to behave a certain way even if we weren't the ones controlling it. Then, they find a way for the Chinese to steal it like they try to do with all our tech. In this case, they used a college kid who Counterintelligence Command had been monitoring for the past couple of years, bringing him into the program as an intern, giving him access, and looking the other way as he ham-fisted his way through making a copy of the program."

Drew's face went white as the admiral's words sunk in. Ish had been working for the Chinese since college. Throughout their entire friendship, he had been a traitor. He had lied to her face about who he was. Her entire world began to close in around her. Although she had known since being chased out of her apartment a few days ago, now there was no denying the truth. Drew barely made it to the trash can before throwing up. She looked up to see Matt kneeling beside her, holding out a box of tissues and a bottle of water.

"Thank you," she said, taking a tissue from the box and the bottle of water.

"Take your time," Matt said.

Once Drew had a chance to compose herself, the admiral continued.

"Apparently, our deception worked, because the Chinese

immediately put the system into operation. Mission accomplished."

"So when and how are we going to use this exploit to our advantage? I would think that this might be a good time to use it before thousands of people die and the Chinese consume their neighbor," Matt asked.

"We did," Admiral Jennings replied. "The system was trained with everything it needed to be Napoleon, Patton, and MacArthur, all in a single package—with one exception. They taught it that red dots on roads represented impassible roadblocks and signaled it to order formations to turn around. The developers ran it through something like ten thousand training events where that was one of the critical features of the terrain, and apparently were convinced the lesson had taken. So, to prepare for the invasion, we had the Vietnamese painting red circles at all of the border crossing points and at major intersections."

"I'm guessing that didn't work?" Matt said.

"Hell no. They rolled right over them without giving it a second chance. Who the hell would ever be fooled by painted dots?"

"The premise makes sense," Drew chimed in, color having returned to her cheeks. "Data poisoning has always been a concern for AI. You basically feed it lies so that it comes to false conclusions. Of course, that's normally done with a completed AI, but there's nothing saying that you couldn't do the same thing when you were building the algorithm itself by manipulating the training data."

"The PLA has just rolled a division directly over that theory," Admiral Jennings retorted.

Drew thought for a moment.

"The two most obvious explanations are either that the team did a poor job of poisoning the training, or that the Chinese found that error and removed it."

"Does it matter?"

"Not for the Vietnamese," she admitted, "but they would only look for something like that in the millions of lines of code if they knew something was there to find. That means Ish wouldn't be the only one working with the Chinese if that was the case. Someone tipped them off."

A second wave of nausea his Drew. The idea that someone else on her team might have been capable of doing something like this. Fortunately, she was able to hold her emotions in check this time instead of spilling them into the trash can.

"I'll let the counterintel folks deal with that," Admiral Jennings said. "For now, though, I've got to figure out how to help General Davis stop the Chinese Patton–Napoleon from taking Hanoi. Thanks for the added information. It's helpful."

The admiral got up from his chair and walked out of the room with his chief of staff in tow. Matt and Drew walked out of the conference room and down the hall to the security office. A young petty officer greeted them from behind a desk and handed them some documents.

"Captain Pink gave me a message, so you just need to read and sign. Everything has already been filled out for you," he said.

After signing the security documentation and nondisclosure agreements, Drew and Matt dropped their temporary badges off with the guards and started walking back up the side of the hill to where the jeep was parked.

"Napoleon wishes he were so lucky," Drew said, slightly out of breath from the steps.

"What do you mean?" Matt asked.

"I mean, Napoleon was a tactical genius, but he had to fumble around in the dark, relying on scouting reports to figure out where the enemy was. Our system doesn't have that problem. It knows everything, thanks to those fancy devices they've been using to decrypt whatever they want."

Matt stopped walking and stared at her. "Shit. I didn't put that together, but that's exactly what they would do, isn't it?"

"That's what I would do. AI's real power comes from being able to consume huge amounts of data, and use everything available to make decisions. Unlike humans, who have come up with mental shortcuts because we just can't deal with that amount of data. Give the most advanced decision-making system on the planet near-perfect information, and it's unstoppable," Drew said. At first, there was a hint of pride behind her words. After all, it was what she had been working toward all her life. Gradually, that pride gave way to dread.

Chapter 15

Sitting on the couch, Frank looked at a picture on the wall of a family whose living room he had just turned into a fighting position, wondering where they were and when they would be able to return to their home. The minutes dragged on as the team waited for any sign of the approaching Chinese vanguard. Growing up, he had heard his father and grandfather talk about the maddening stillness before an expected firefight. He hadn't understood what they were saying, because it seemed to be at odds with how they talked about the deafening violence that surrounded them in an engagement. Now, waiting for an unknown but certainly larger, better-equipped force, Frank began to see. It was the uncertainty that was getting to him. Would the Chinese forces show up? When? How many troops? Would his plan work? Would he bring all his team home tonight? The more Frank sat with these questions, the more he wished for something to happen.

Lieutenant Nguyen's phone vibrated, jolting Frank out of his own head. Reading the message, the lieutenant turned to Frank. "Sergeant Giap has reported movement along the roadway. It is too far away to discern specific vehicles, but he indicates that it is a significant force."

"Look alive," Frank said over the team radio. "The OP just

spotted a tactical column headed our way."

Frank looked over to Lieutenant Nguyen and nodded. The wait was almost over. At least that part, because now Frank had to continue waiting for another ten minutes before the large vehicles began rumbling in the distance. The team continued to wait as the sound grew closer and louder. Finally, Frank saw the front end of a tank roll around the corner, stopping just short of the bridge.

"Hold your fire until it gets into the kill zone. We initiate with the IEDs," Frank transmitted, quickly echoed in Vietnamese by Lieutenant Nguyen.

The tank stood still while a team of infantry moved up alongside it, taking cover behind the guardrails at the end of the bridge. Then Frank watched as four small tracked vehicles armed with heavy machine guns rolled into place next to the dismounted infantry. Once the drones stopped, the tank began creeping forward onto the bridge. It got half of the hull onto the span before stopping abruptly.

"What's it doing?" Mac asked.

"Not sure," Frank replied. "We've got enough standoff from the windows that even with advanced optics they should be able to see us."

From behind the lead tank, a second moved off the road and took up a position to the right of the bridge. Frank saw both turrets begin to move in unison. The hair on the back of his neck stood up. Something was wrong. He keyed the radio, but before he could say anything, the riverbank erupted. Both tanks opened fire with their main guns, each targeting one of the two houses the team was hiding in. When they did, the dismounted infantry and drones also began firing.

The roof above Frank exploded, showering everyone inside

with wood and chunks of roof tile. Everyone fell to the floor. Regaining his composure, Lieutenant Nguyen crawled up to the window and began returning fire as a hail of bullets peppered the side of the building. Following his example, the rest of the Rangers also got into the fight.

"We've been made. We've got to withdraw," Frank shouted into his radio. "We're not going to win a gunfight with a tank division."

Crouching below the level of the window, Frank moved up next to Lieutenant Nguyen, and motioned for him to have his platoon collapse back. The lieutenant nodded and issued the order over their radio. Despite the complete and utter chaos consuming the entire building, the platoon withdrew exactly as they had practiced endlessly on the range a few weeks earlier. The gun team displaced, covered by the riflemen, who followed immediately behind them out of the building. Frank gave one final look around the room to make sure they didn't leave anything critical behind and raced to catch up.

No sooner had he reached the doorway, than the entire building exploded as a second tank round sailed through the window and impacted into the inner wall dividing the living room from the kitchen. Frank was thrown forward out of the home and landed in the grass five feet away. Partially exposed to the enemy fire streaking down the road, he jumped up and rushed backward, using several parked cars as cover. In moments, he had covered the distance between the first and second rows of houses, and rushed inside.

"I'm the last one," Frank shouted to Rizzo and the team, who had been covering their movement. "Let's get out of here."

Rizzo gave him a thumbs-up and began rounding up everyone in the building. Frank ran back outside and around the far end of the building to where the team had staged their vehicles. Tim was already in the driver's seat and the engine was started. Around him, Green Berets and Rangers were loading into the vehicles, and firing out of the windows to cover the movement of those still retreating.

"Mount up. We need to get the hell out of here now," Frank said. "Rizzo, Tyler, watch the kill zones. If that tank comes across, blow it. We still might have a chance to slow them down. Give me an up when you have everyone."

"One up."

"Two up."

"Three up."

"We have all loaded," Lieutenant Nguyen said.

"All right, get us the hell out of here, Tim," Frank said.

Gravel scattered out from underneath the car's tires as Tim accelerated hard onto the dirt path that paralleled the main road, avoiding the tank's line of sight. Ten seconds later, Frank heard an explosion and saw a cloud of dust and debris rise from the center of the bridge, totally obscuring the engagement area. Craning his neck out of the window as the dust cleared, Frank saw two drones turned on their sides, destroyed in the blast. A third drone was missing a track but still advancing slowly. Its exposed road wheels slipping on the concrete, the drone began drifting to the left. Suddenly the tank's massive tread rolled right on top of the drone, unceremoniously crushing it as the driver raced to reach the safety at the far side of the bridge.

Safely out of the kill zone on the bridge, the tank picked up speed in an attempt to catch the fleeing team. As it drove between the two buildings, another series of explosions went off. Tyler had timed the secondary charges perfectly. When the dust cleared again, the tank sat motionless in the middle of the road between the two half-destroyed houses. Now back racing along the highway, Frank kept his eyes on the tank for as long as possible. Just before it went out of view, he saw the hatch pop open and a soldier stumble out. They may not have completely shut the road off on the bridge, but the Chinese column would be slowed down while they dealt with the disabled tank blocking the path.

The team drove back to their compound at Bac Kan as fast as possible. Most of the traffic they had seen going to Khanh Khe had died down as people had finished evacuating, but the road was still littered with vehicles, suitcases, and boxes that had been left behind. The pleasant drive through the countryside the team had made multiple times before had been transformed by the unmistakable marks of panic.

While helping Tim navigate, Frank spent his time trying to find out what was going on from the news sources available on his phone, but the lack of reliable cell service made that mostly impossible. From the back seat, Lieutenant Nguyen cycled through his contact list, calling everyone he knew for updated information. Despite their best efforts, neither was able to come up with any clear picture of how the attack was progressing. From what they could tell, the Chinese had come across the border at three points, with a fourth point possible. The Chinese assault had advanced steadily for the first several hours but was now meeting stronger resistance at hasty defensive positions set up by the Vietnamese army, augmented by the local police force. It was unclear if those defensive positions were strong enough to hold, or if they would simply serve to delay the attack long enough for Vietnamese forces to mass more combat power forward.

Frank was a little surprised by the slow response from the American military, which seemed to be caused at least in some part by the change of leadership at INDOPACOM. It was odd, he thought, that the DOD would change its senior leader out during a crisis. Once back at their compound, he could contact SOCPAC on a secure line and find out more about what was really going on.

The team pulled into the compound. A trip that would normally have taken three hours had turned into ten, and Frank couldn't wait to peel himself from the passenger seat. Getting out of the vehicle and stretching, he looked around at the rest of the team and tried to gauge their morale.

"Well, that could have gone better," Mike said, walking up from the rear vehicle. "But it could also have gone way worse. Thank God we didn't lose anybody."

"Yeah. There's something about the way that went down that has been bothering me the whole ride back. That lead tank stopped suddenly when it was rolling up on the bridge like it caught sight of something, but the angle of the incline meant that its optics weren't actually on us when it jerked to a halt. Even if we were visible somehow, which we weren't, it wasn't in any position to actually see us. How did it know?"

"Good question. We can add it to the list of things to ask the S2 when we get them on the phone. I'd recommend not staying in this place much longer, though. If the Chinese manage to break through the initial defenses, which is highly likely, this place is in line to get overrun next."

"I concur with your assessment, Chief Smith," Lieutenant Nguyen said. "We have already completed most of the preparation to leave, but will finish doing so now. We should be prepared to move within the hour."

"Good," Frank said. "Mike, let's make sure we're ready to roll too. I'll run comms off of my cellular router so Eli can pack up his kit."

The three men split up, and Frank headed to the command post. He walked through the door and set his body armor and rifle on the floor. Turning toward the corner where his computer was set up, he jumped at the sight of a man already sitting in his chair.

"Captain Gonzales," the man said, standing up and walking toward him with an outstretched hand. "I'm Major Matt Anderson. I need your help."

Frank looked the stranger over and shook his hand. "Nice to meet you, sir," Frank said. "You picked a hell of a time to show up."

"Don't I know it," Matt said.

The door to the CP opened. Mike stepped through and did a double take at the sight of the unexpected visitor.

"Frank, who is this, and why is he in our CP?" Mike asked.

"I'm Major Matt Anderson," Matt repeated. "I'm with the unit out of Washington, and I'm here because I need your help."

Frank saw an immediate change in Mike's demeanor from Matt's explanation, even though it hadn't actually clarified anything for Frank.

"What unit? The Pentagon?" Frank asked.

"No, Frank," Mike interjected. "Matt isn't some random staffer. He's one of us. What can we do to help you, sir?"

"You sent in a report about some sort of kinetic or EW device that a Chinese covert cell brought across the border and emplaced in a local telecom office. I need you to take me there."

Eli walked into the CP, wheeling a plastic case behind him.

He walked around the three men talking, giving Matt a quizzical look, and began packing up the remaining communications equipment.

"Sir, I'd really like to help, but we don't have a lot of time to spare here," Frank said. "We just got our asses handed to us by one of the Chinese columns heading this way, and they are going to be here sooner rather than later."

"What happened?" Matt asked.

"We set up an ambush at a bridge east of here to delay their advance. We had everything set up, but then it all went to shit."

"What do you mean by that?"

"I mean the lead tank started rolling up onto the bridge and directly into our kill zone, but then it suddenly stopped like it realized we were there. It called up its wingman and they blew us out of our ambush positions."

"Were you spotted?" Matt probed.

"No," Frank said with a healthy dose of indignation. "Our position was good. They wouldn't have been able to see us. Especially with how the vehicle's hull was angled. If they would have seen us, they wouldn't have moved partially onto the bridge."

"I see. When it started rolling, did you do any final check with your team to make sure everyone was ready?"

"Of course I did. We had to keep everyone on the line calm and remind them not to open fire until the explosives went off."

"Gentlemen, that's why I am here, and that's why I need your help. That thing you saw installed in the telecom office was an advanced decryption device that gives the Chinese instant access to every bit of information moving in and around the telecommunications infrastructure. Paired with their other electronic-warfare sensing capabilities, like the one that probably detected your radio signals, they hear and know everything that is transmitted electronically."

"Even if that was true, there's no way they could actually process, analyze, and disseminate information at a speed that would translate that into tactical action like we saw," Mike pushed back.

"They can when they've paired it with an advanced AI system and given over near-total control of their formations to it. It detected your signal, discovered the threat, and relayed new instructions to the tank crew. All in a fraction of a second, and it could do that along every axis of advance simultaneously without breaking a sweat."

"Sir, if that's true, it's probably the most terrifying thing I've ever heard," Frank said. "How the hell are we supposed to mount any sort of cogent defense against that sort of information dominance? Even if we were evenly matched that would be a tall order, and you want us to take them on with what? One ODA and a platoon of Vietnamese Rangers?"

"No, the Vietnamese army will worry about fighting those battles. I need your help to win the war."

"What's your plan?" Mike asked.

"Well, first thing is relocating. I've got a team house getting set up east of Hanoi that should be big enough for both you and your Ranger counterparts. We should leave as soon as possible. You'll have to leave all of your cell phones, though. I'm sure it's tagged all of the electronics you had with you at the bridge. Since it owns the network, it can track your movement and keep tabs on what you're doing. Even if it can't reach you yet, best not to give it any more information than necessary. Once we get set up in the new team house, we can start making a plan to take out its surveillance nodes."

"There's more than one?" Frank asked.

"I don't know. I've confirmed the one you saw installed, but it's safe to assume there are multiple. I've got analysts working to locate any others."

"I'm going to need to run this by my command first. I still haven't checked in with them since we pulled off the bridge," Frank said, powering up his computer and sliding on his headset.

"Do what you have to. Just know that everything you say, even though it's running through a Type I encryption device, is going to be instantly heard."

Frank looked at Matt, sizing him up, and slowly pulled the headset off. "I guess we're on our own, then. We've got another problem, though. We're not outfitted for any of this. We were here on a JCET, and just burned through almost all of our ammo during that ambush. We were supposed to get a resupply, but now I'm not sure if it's actually going to get here."

Matt smiled. "How do you think I got here? I've got your two containers already staged. Plus, I brought some more things I think we might need, courtesy of Admiral Jennings. We can talk more later, but now we need to get you all out of here."

Chapter 16

Matt stepped down from the Land Cruiser and walked back to the opening he had just come through. Once the trail vehicle drove inside, he pulled down the door. The clang of the thin sheet-metal door echoed across the large, empty warehouse as it came to rest on the concrete floor.

"Welcome to your new home," Matt said, walking up to Frank and Lieutenant Nguyen. "Your two containers are the ones on the left there, but all of that stuff is for you. I've got all my gear in my truck. One of those containers has a couple HF radios in it. For now, that's probably about the best thing we have to coordinate with SOCPAC, if you want to get your echo working on standing that up. There's a ladder for roof access out back. Once you two get your teams working on establishing this site, we can come back together and start making our plan."

"You said that it was able to pick up our transmissions," Frank said.

"HF is different. The way it works makes it exceedingly difficult to detect a signal, and even if they do manage to pick it up, tracing it back to its source is next to impossible. It's not as quick to set up, and our bandwidth will be limited to small messages, but it keeps whatever we say out of enemy hands."

Twenty minutes later, Matt had a whiteboard set up on a small table leaning against his truck, along with his computer, opened up to mapping software. He was zooming in and out on different areas, trying to get a sense for the terrain.

"I thought connecting any electronics was a bad idea," Frank said, walking over to him.

"It is," Matt replied. "This computer isn't connected to anything. I downloaded some updated map files before I took off from Hawaii so I'd have some sort of imagery to go off of. If you're ready, grab your LT and warrant and let's talk."

Frank let out a whistle to get Mike's attention, and he and Lieutenant Nguyen came over.

"All right, first tell me about what you saw and where you saw it," Matt said.

"The cell we were watching linked up with a truck near the border two nights ago. They transferred a heavy case that was maybe two feet by two feet by one foot deep into the back of their car, and then drove it to an office in Lang Son. They brought the case into the building, and came out about an hour or so later. When they did, though, the case was obviously lighter, so they clearly left whatever it was inside the building."

"Show me where in Lang Son the building is, please."

Frank used the mouse to scroll in on the imagery and centered it on the large white building. "That's it," he said.

"All right, look. As long as that device, or any others like it, is active, the Chinese have an all-seeing eye. We have to take it out for the Vietnamese forces to have any chance. Frank, LT—this is still your unit. I don't know how you all fight, so I won't try to come in and take over that part. I just need you to get me inside the building and into the server room so that we can destroy the system. That's the objective. Can you do that?"

Lieutenant Nguyen eyed the building for a moment and then picked up a marker. "Yes, Major, I believe we can. We will have to assume that Lang Son will already be under enemy control, so must be very deliberate in our planning of the approach. Nevertheless, we will find a way."

Matt sat back and watched as the three men started drafting their plan. Drawing a rough sketch of the imagery onto the board, they talked through multiple different ways to approach and enter the building. Erasing and redrawing isolation, overwatch, and assault elements, the three men iterated through their options until all three were happy with what they had. They redrew their sketch cleanly on the edge of the whiteboard and repeated the process to work through how to move to their objective and how to get back across the front line safely. Once they had their complete plan together, they called the team together and talked through the mission.

"Sir," Eli said, walking up to Frank after the mission briefing was over, "I've got the HF radio up and tethered to my laptop. If you want to send an update it's ready."

"Thanks, Eli. Matt, need to pass anything along to SOC-PAC?" Frank asked.

"Just tell 'em what we're planning to do. No need to belabor the point."

Frank nodded and sat down in front of Eli's laptop.

ODA 1312 SITREP. Ambush at Khanh Khe bridge likely unsuccessful in stopping that axis of advance. Linked up with MAJ Anderson. Relocated, regrouped, and rearmed. Planning attack of communications node in Lang Son. Request additional resupply as practicable—ammunition and batteries of highest priority. Please send intelligence updates as available.

Frank hit Send and watched as the system transmitted the message and confirmed receipt. Closing the laptop, he stood up and started preparing his individual kit for the operation—reloading magazines, changing out batteries, and refilling the water.

Looking around the warehouse, Matt saw two squads going through rehearsals, another doing a gear check, and a fourth preparing their vehicles. The Green Berets were similarly engaged with their own preparations, with the exception of one, who was helping one of the Ranger squads with their rehearsal. Matt was impressed by the team's focus and attention to detail. If there was a team currently in the country that could pull this off, he assessed that they were it.

As the evening wore on, the activity died down. Preparations complete, soldiers began stretching out on the floor to catch what little sleep they could. They wanted to time their attack for the darkest part of the night, so they had five hours before they had to leave. Following their lead, Matt crawled into the back of his truck and pulled his hat over his eyes.

Three hours later, Matt woke up and climbed out of the back of his truck. He saw Frank sitting in front of the computer and went over to join him.

"How are we looking, Frank?" Matt said, sitting down in the chair beside him.

"Good, sir."

"My name is Matt, Frank. SOCPAC able to come back with anything interesting?"

"The Vietnamese are doing the best they can. They've had isolated success holding back the main three axes of advance, but it's mostly just delaying actions. SOCPAC's best estimate is that the Vietnamese will need about three more days before they can launch a counteroffensive. Until then, local troops, augmented by the police, are going to continue doing the best they can to keep slowing the advance down until the main resistance can arrive."

"What about US support?" Matt asked.

"They're preparing a joint task force, but it's not going to be here for a while. SOCPAC requested an O6 headquarters and a battalion to come out and help advise and assist. The Air Force is also working to bring in additional ISR assets to help us better understand the threat."

"None of which is going to help us for the next week at least," Matt said. "The cavalry isn't coming. It's just us. Let's start getting everyone up and ready to move."

Frank woke up Mike and Rizzo. Lieutenant Nguyen was already awake, and got his platoon moving as well. In an hour, the entire team was walking through the plan one last time. Preparations complete, the team loaded into the vehicles and headed out of the warehouse.

Once outside the limits of Hanoi's urban sprawl, the team found they had the roads mostly to themselves, although several checkpoints and defensive positions had begun to pop up. Unsure of exactly where the vanguard of the Chinese attack was, the team was sticking to the smaller side roads and gravel paths. One of the Vietnamese riflemen, who had grown up in this area, helped guide the convoy north.

After six hours of cautious driving, the team reached the southern edge of Lang Son, marked by a police checkpoint. Lieutenant Nguyen got out of his vehicle and approached the four men standing guard. Five minutes later, he walked back to Frank's car. Matt hopped out of his Land Cruiser to hear what the lieutenant had learned. Gunfire echoed in the distance, reminding him of how close to the front they now stood.

"The enemy has advanced into the north part of the city. Elements from the first division are holding their defensive positions, thanks in large part to the timely arrival of some antitank missiles. There are reports of Chinese reconnaissance units working to find alternate paths into the city, but it seems that they do not wish to simply bypass the area."

"Who controls the area around our building?" Matt asked.

"From the soldier's description, that terrain may already belong to the enemy."

"Well, that certainly complicates things," Frank said.

"Yes, but it does not make it impossible. I think the route we have selected has a high probability of getting us to the location undetected."

"Detection is one thing," Matt said. "That communications node is one of the most critical pieces of terrain in the country right now. They might try to downplay its importance to avoid painting it as a target, but if they suspect it could come under attack, they would likely throw everything they had to defend."

"We must hope, then, that our plan is not discovered. The soldier said that our pathway to the selected transition point should be clear, but I would still recommend caution," Lieutenant Nguyen added.

"Let's get to it, then," Frank said.

Lieutenant Nguyen's vehicle assumed the lead position and traveled well ahead of the rest of the convoy. Deliberately picking their path to avoid roads with long, straight sections where they could be observed from a distance, he led the team into a parking lot. The team backed their vehicles up against the south-facing concrete wall of a grocery store and got out. As they did, Sergeant Tran took control of one of the rifle squads emplacing them as security around the site. The rest of the team worked through their final precombat checks, preparing their kit for night operations as the sun fell behind the buildings.

"Keep one of your radios on. They're going to pick up any transmissions, though, so don't use it until absolutely necessary. We'll do the same," Rizzo reiterated to Sergeant Tran.

"We will follow the plan, and see you back here," Sergeant Tran said, slapping his American counterpart on the shoulder.

Rizzo smiled, and the two began counting the soldiers as they stepped off into the night. Matt took his place toward the back of the formation. Despite the persistent audible reminder of fighting up ahead, he was surprised at the relatively small number of larger explosions from artillery or rockets. He wondered if China was purposely trying to preserve as much of the civilian infrastructure as possible, or if Lang Son was getting special treatment because of the presence of the device.

The team stretched out along both sides of the narrow roads as they made their way north. Three blocks away from the building, they ducked into an abandoned garage.

"We're across the street from the target building," Frank said to the leaders huddled in the center of the room. "Mike, you and Mac get the overwatch set up, and kick out the security elements. The assault team is going to launch from here once you all are good to go. It seems like the fighting is still several hundred meters north of us, so it's likely that we won't encounter any resistance. Anyone have any last-minute concerns?"

Frank looked around the circle, making eye contact with everyone. Matt gave him a nod, and the group broke up. Mac called in the Ranger squad leaders and divided up the security sectors while the assault element made their final preparations. Matt watched as Tyler prepared two breaching charges in case they needed help gaining entry into the building. Standing at the rear entrance leading out from the back of the garage directly opposite the telecom building, Frank took a deep breath and opened the door.

The two Vietnamese Ranger squads ran out the door with the Green Berets on their heels. The team crossed the road at an all-out sprint and threw themselves against the wall of the building just to the left of the double glass doors of the front entrance. Pausing long enough for the lead fire team to stack up next to the door, another rifleman stepped forward with a sledgehammer and slammed it through the glass. Matt wasn't sure that the shattered remnants of the door had even hit the ground before the Rangers burst into the building.

As soon as the third man crossed the threshold, the lobby exploded into chaos as a machine gun opened up on the team from within the building. The Rangers returned fire, and four seconds later a grenade went off. Matt crashed through the door with the second squad of Rangers. The first squad was set up on both sides of a hallway leading back away from the lobby, laying down a concentrated wall of fire. One Ranger lay on the ground, but before Matt could do anything about it the platoon's medic rushed around him and pulled the injured man back to relative safety behind the front security desk.

Two more grenades went off, and the Rangers were moving down the corridor, continuing to fire down the hallway to keep it clear of any defenders. From his position crouched along the back wall of the lobby, Matt heard the lead element call out and saw the second squad rush down the hallway, followed quickly by Green Berets. More gunshots and three more grenades. Matt moved to the corner of the hallway and poked his head around. At the end of the hall, Matt could see two Rangers kneeling at a T intersection. Moving up to their location, he patted one on the shoulder to let the man know he was there. Around the next corner, Matt saw two bodies sprawled on the floor, with one more halfway through a door off to the left. He turned around and saw four more bodies at the other end of the hall. After a minute of doing his best to avoid looking at the blood pooling underneath the dead defenders, Matt heard a shout from down the hallway. One of the riflemen patted him on the arm and motioned down the hallway.

Matt got up and walked to a doorway where two other Rangers were standing. They got out of his way, and Matt walked in.

"We got you here. Where is this thing?" Frank said, sweat dripping down his face.

"Let's take a look. Did you all find any external coolers or fans or anything?" Matt asked.

"Sir," Tim called, "take a look down here."

Near the center of the room along the back wall, Matt saw three fans and a portable air-conditioning unit, all pointing to a specific spot in one of the server racks. As he got closer, he saw what he was looking for—it was exactly like the others.

"This is it," he called out. Standing next to it, he could tell it hadn't been on long enough to generate as much heat as the one he'd found in Hawaii. He reached into his pocket, pulled out a screwdriver, and unscrewed the device from the rack.

"If they don't already know we're here, they will certainly know as soon as I pull the plug from this thing. Best get everyone prepared to move," he said, removing the last of the mounting screws holding it in place. Matt pulled the power cable from the wall, slid the device from the rack, and zipped it into his duffel bag. "I've got what we came for. Let's get out of here."

Lieutenant Nguyen signaled his squad leaders, and the assault team pulled back from their defensive positions and headed toward the front of the building. Pausing to consolidate in the lobby, the two squad leaders gave a thumbs-up when they had accounted for everyone. As the team moved back across the street to the garage, Matt saw one of the Rangers carrying the wounded man on his back, a tourniquet visible on the man's right thigh.

This time, the team barely broke stride, making their way through the garage and out onto the opposite street. Frank had opted to take a less direct route to their objective, but the way back was almost a direct shot to the vehicles. Driving south out of town, Matt could hear the intensity of fighting to the north increase, augmented by the sound of incoming artillery. Their mission had been a success: they'd captured another device intact, with only a single soldier wounded in the process. Seeing the glow of fires rising in his rear view mirror, though, Matt knew that this team wasn't going to be the ones who paid for their victory tonight.

Chapter 17

Drew woke up with her cheek welded to the arm she had been using for a pillow. Lifting her head off of the desk, she brushed the hair out of her face and tried to shake the weariness away. She looked at her watch: a solid two hours of sleep. More importantly, in about an hour Dirk would walk through the door. She hoped he would be bringing both breakfast and news from Matt. Ever since Matt had left for Vietnam, Drew had holed herself up in the lab with Dirk and his team as they tried to figure out anything they could about the device—how it worked, how to copy it, how to defeat it.

Dirk's original plan had been to pack it up and ship it off to one of the NSA's support labs on the east coast, but once China invaded Vietnam that plan went out the window. Instead, NSA Hawaii became the epicenter of the universe, as the powers that be didn't want to waste any time or risk damaging the device in transit. So the East Coast came to them. At least virtually. At first, questions were raised about why some newly minted intern was involved in the project, but thankfully Dirk shut that down.

In addition to keeping the thing on the island, the war also motivated the NSA to authorize all resources available to exploit it. She and Dirk had spent all day yesterday tweaking one of their tools to break into the solid-state drives. Drew had finished writing the program shortly after midnight, and hadn't waited for approval to start running it. She pushed herself upright and looked at her computer screen: still processing. Hopping down from the stool, Drew walked to the coffeepot. Swirling the remaining contents around, she decided that a fresh cup would be better than whatever dregs remained, so she went down the hall to refill the water. She placed the new filter, added twelve heaping tablespoons of the finest coffee the government could buy, and hit the button. Her spine started to wake up with the machine's first gurgles.

Returning to her desk to check her messages, Drew saw that the program had finished. As she navigated through the command prompt, she let out a yelp of excitement.

"What's that all about?" Dirk asked, standing in the doorway with a breakfast burrito wrapped in aluminum foil.

"It worked! We're in!" she shouted.

Dirk rushed over to stand next to her, nearly knocking her off of the stool. "Show me."

Drew quickly talked him through the rest of the code she had written the night before, and the two of them began scrolling through the results.

"Hold on a minute. Let me get my computer so we can both go through this at the same time. While you're waiting, eat that burrito. God knows the last time you ate something." Dirk ran out of the lab toward his office.

When he returned a few minutes later, he found Drew working on her breakfast and reading the walls of text on her screen. He set his laptop down and poured two cups of coffee. Handing one to Drew, he smiled. "What did we find?"

"I'm still not totally sure. So far, it's mostly a bunch of typical boot files and startup logs. I think I just haven't found the good stuff yet."

"It's there. Has to be. I'll spin up some of our external analytics servers and get them to run our top three exploitation scripts. These drives aren't that big, though, so it really shouldn't take that long for them to get through."

"Any word from Matt?" Drew asked.

"No, but I wouldn't be too worried about that. Matt's one of the most gifted guys I've ever met. He'll never admit it, but he ran circles around all of us growing up. I mean, I'm doing well for myself here at the NSA, competing with some of the brightest minds in the country, but with him it wasn't even close. If there's a way, he'll find it."

For the next several hours, Drew and Dirk continued working to unravel the inner workings of the device. As additional engineers and data scientists joined in, Dirk assigned them different lines of effort, acting as both traffic cop and lead detective. Feeling that she had hit a dead end with her current path, Drew decided it was best if she actually left the lab for a moment—for her own sanity. And to take a shower—for everyone else's sake. She checked out with Dirk and told him she was going to shower and take a quick nap back at her hotel room.

She walked out of the building, blinded by the tropical sunlight. Driving back down toward the water, she was struck by how weird it was that thousands of people were crawling all over this island having the time of their lives, blissfully unaware that a war was going on, and that it likely wasn't going well for their side. Two weeks earlier, that would have been her.

She turned the shower on and stripped out of her clothes

while it heated up. In the background, a news anchor mono-logued on the TV about how bravely the Vietnamese defenders were fighting for their homelands against the Chinese hordes. As polished and confident as the anchor sounded, Drew couldn't help but think that he was just about as removed from the news he was reporting as the beachgoers outside her bedroom window. Stepping under the water, she did her best not to think about it, lest it overwhelm her. She stared off into space and tried to block out everything but the water running down her back. Despite her best efforts, though, Drew couldn't block it out. She couldn't shut out the world that she now knew existed. She shut the water off and stepped out onto the bathmat. Toweling her hair, she was struck with an idea. At first, it was just a whisper in the back of her mind, barely perceptible, but by the time she had put on a fresh set of clothes it had fully taken hold. Drew rushed out of her room, nearly forgetting the keys to the rental car, and ran down the hallway to the stairs.

-

Matt watched as the small jet taxied to a stop at the edge of the ramp. As the plane spun down its engines, the door dropped open, and Drew came bounding down the stairs.

"That was literally the coolest thing I have ever done in my entire life," she said, walking over to Matt and giving him a hug. "I need to become super famous or something, because there's no way I can ever fly normally again."

"Nice flight, I take it?" Matt asked.

One of the crew rolled two suitcases around and passed them to Matt. Taking the handles, he rolled them behind him as he led Drew to where his Land Cruiser was parked, just off the tarmac.

"How are you doing?" she asked.

"We're still getting our asses handed to us," Matt said, putting the truck in drive and pulling onto the main road. "I thought taking that device out of play was going to really set them back, but it doesn't seem to have had the level of impact I would have liked. Once the PLA got their initial footing, they really started picking up steam. If they stay on this pace, Hanoi will fall in a matter of days. Most of the government has already relocated south to Da Nang, but the prime minister and defense minister have vowed to stay and fight. I'm beginning to think that there's another system out there. Why wouldn't they employ multiple systems?"

"My analysts checked. Based on all of the data they have available, which is pretty much all of it now that the Vietnamese government is helping, there isn't another device in Vietnam. I'm not sure there has to be, though. Even if we successfully removed their ability to read our mail, they still have a genius AI that has all the information available to it that the Chinese intelligence apparatus can muster—which, now that I'm read on to such things, is a lot. But that's why I'm here."

"I'm still not sure that this plan is going to work."

"Neither am I," Drew admitted. "But it's the best option we have given the tools we have available. Your old plans no longer fit the current enemy. It's time to adapt."

"I hope you're right," Matt said.

Drew's eyes were glued to the window as Matt made his way northeast. Even if she wished it were under different circumstances, she couldn't help but feeling a sense of awe at how beautiful the country was. And different. After several hours of driving, he pulled into the warehouse and backed his truck toward a wall alongside another vehicle.

"Here we are. Home sweet home," he said, stepping onto the concrete slab.

Following him out of the vehicle, she looked around the large open interior of the warehouse. "I love what you've done with the place. It has a barndominium look with a heavy-industrial vibe. I dig it."

"Only the best for me," Matt smiled, opening the back of the Land Cruiser and pulling out Drew's two bags.

"I only need the gray one. The blue one just has clothes in it," she said.

Rolling the suitcase behind him, Matt led Drew to a corner of the warehouses where several tables had been set up.

"Eli, this is Drew Drum," Matt said. "Drew, this is Sergeant First Class Eli Montgomery. He's one of the team's communications sergeants."

Eli stood and offered Drew his hand. "Welcome to Hanoi," he said. "Matt said you're an expert in this new toy of ours."

"If staring at it longer than anyone else makes me an expert, then sure. Let's go with that," she said, shaking Eli's hand.

"When is the rest of the team due back, Eli?" Matt asked.

"The main element should be back from their recon in an hour or so. Rizzo and Sergeant Tran might be a few hours later from a supply run."

"What do you need from us, Drew?" Matt asked. "Best we can tell, it was only online for two or three days, so it should have plenty of life left if we can get it back online."

"We won't need to power on the main system until we actually install it. Until then, there's a subsystem we found that will let us get what we need," Drew said, taking off her backpack and lifting the suitcase onto the table. She pulled a small hard drive from the suitcase and handed it to Matt. "This drive should have the intelligence data you asked for. Dirk said to tell you that now that you have this it will be easier for SOCPAC to feed you updated files to keep your intel picture current."

"Thanks. I'm going to go comb through this and see what they've sent us. Are you good here?"

Drew nodded, pulled her laptop out of her bag, and started working. She was so lost in her work that Matt startled her when he put his hand on her shoulder sometime later.

"Sorry," he said, "I didn't mean to make you jump. I wanted to introduce you to Captain Frank Gonzales, ODA team leader, and Lieutenant Nguyen Nam, platoon leader from the Second Ranger Battalion."

"Pleasure to meet you both." Drew said, standing up from her chair.

"Good afternoon, miss," Lieutenant Nguyen said.

"Gentlemen," Matt said, "I've been busy since you've been gone. I think I found what we're looking for. I'd like to start planning how we're going to pull this off."

"I'll go grab Mike," Frank said.

The four men stood around the whiteboard and Matt's computer, talking through the plan. An hour into their planning session, Rizzo and Sergeant Tran returned with three truckloads of supplies—including some hot food from a local restaurant.

"You've returned!" Mike smiled as Rizzo walked up to the group.

"And I come bearing the best gift of all," Rizzo said, holding up the bags of food.

"You know how to treat a guy right," Mike said. "If Diane ever kicks me out of the house, I can tell you where I'm coming."

While Rizzo handed out the containers of food, Frank filled him in. The men continued to talk as they ate, and by the time they had finished their meal, they had a plan together. Matt left the group as they brought in the rest of the team to brief their plan, and walked over to where Drew was working.

"You forgot to get your dinner," he said, sliding a plate of chicken and rice onto the table. "How's it going?"

"Thank you. Ish would always have to . . ." Drew's expression dropped. "I used to forget to eat all the time. Especially when big projects were due." She took the plate and started eating. After a minute, she looked back up at Matt. "What's going to happen to him?"

"To Ish?"

"Yeah," she said softly.

"I don't know for sure, but none of the ways these things usually play out end up in Ish's favor."

Drew stabbed at her food, unsure about how to respond. Eventually, she decided to change the subject. "I think this is going to work. I've got the operating system updated and most of the configuration complete. I think I'll be finished up with my part in another couple of hours."

"Perfect. We'll be ready to roll by nightfall. We're going to drop you off at the consulate on our way out."

"The hell you are. What if something goes wrong when you get there? Who's going to troubleshoot the system and bring it back online?"

"I'm not taking you with us. There's a high likelihood that we're going to get into some sort of trouble, and I won't put you in danger."

"Don't be ridiculous. I won't be in any more danger than you. Do you want this plan to work, or don't you?"

"You have no idea how the quantum system works," Matt said, raising his voice slightly.

"I know a hell of a lot more than you. And I know how the rest of the system works. Definitely better than you. Take your notions of chivalry and file it under 'things that will make this fail.' I'm coming." Drew glared at Matt.

"Have you ever fired a weapon before?"

Drew smiled, recognizing she had won. "I brought down an eight-point last year with my uncle."

Matt raised an eyebrow. "Not many hunting rifles available. Probably better if we just stick with a pistol. I'll see if Tim or Gary has an extra they can spare."

"Good. Now if you don't mind, I need to get back to work."

Matt went back toward where the team was assembled. Drew sat down, but before she got back to work, she turned to watch him walking away.

-

"It's worse than we thought up ahead," Mike said, leaning out of his window. Matt had pulled his Land Cruiser up alongside Mike's Hilux so that they could talk. "We're still three kilometers from our planned vehicle-staging point, but I don't think we can risk going any further."

"OK, Mike," Matt said. "We'll just drop the vehicles here and go the rest of the way on foot. It's not ideal, but we don't really have any other choice. Do you think we can make some progress on foot before nightfall, or are we going to be too exposed up there?"

"I think we can make it part of the way, but we won't want to get too far up toward the front until night."

The team pulled their vehicles off of the road, parking them out of sight behind the thick vegetation. Checking their gear one last time, they shouldered their rucks and got ready to move. Matt looked over at Tim, who had the unenviable task of carrying the device in his pack. The weight and awkwardness of the load didn't seem to even register to the man. Mac and Sergeant Van, the Rangers' first-squad leader, counted each man out as they started their approach.

Silently picking their way through the landscape, the team made their way through the forest before breaking out in the light residential area that lined the valley below the Thac Ba Reservoir. Despite the calm that surrounded them in this quiet neighborhood, the occasional explosion of artillery in the distance was a constant reminder of just how close they were to the front. To make matters worse, they were on the wrong side of it.

Taking rutted back roads and single-track dirt paths, they had gone around the main avenues of approach and slipped in behind the Chinese advance. Although they had bypassed the units at the front, there was still a danger of running into ones moving up to reinforce the main advance or security patrols intent on preventing units from slipping around behind and disrupting their operation, which was exactly what they were doing. An hour before sunrise, they reached their destination.

Matt moved up from the rear of the formation, bringing Drew with him. He found Mac and kneeled next to him.

"Is this the place?" Matt whispered.

"Yep. Sergeant Van says the entrance to the dam control

facility is across the street there," Mac replied.

"OK. Let's see about getting inside." Matt ran across the street to the front door of the building and slid off his ruck. Reaching inside, he pulled out his lockpick set to open the outer doors. Two Rangers knelt a few feet away from him, watching down the road. Reaching for the knob, Matt found that it turned in his hand.

"Looks like they forgot to lock the place up when they left," he said. Placing the picks back in his bag, he waved Mac over. "We're in."

Quickly, the team moved into the building, leaving the street outside quiet once again. The squad of Rangers cleared through the structure to make sure there were no surprises. After they were sure there was no one in the building, they began setting up security positions. Since they were behind the Chinese line, staying undetected was their best defensive strategy. Matt and Drew waited until Mac gave them the all-clear signal, and then made their way down the hall to one of the mechanical rooms.

"This isn't it. It's just HVAC in here. Let's try another," Matt said as he moved out into the corridor. After looking through two more rooms, they found the one they were looking for.

"Bingo," he said. "This should be the main transmission room for the facility. We can pull power off of this distribution box and plug directly into the hard line that provides connectivity to the plant's autonomous control system. That should give us the internet access we're looking for. Both the Vietnamese and Chinese know how bad it could be if this dam stops functioning properly, so we'll have all the power and connectivity we need. Wait here and I'll grab Tim."

Drew slid a small table closer to the access point's router and opened her laptop. Matt returned a minute later with Tim, who pulled the device out of his bag and set it on the table.

"Thanks, Tim," Matt said.

"Sure. Let me know if you need any more help. I'll just be out making sure the security positions are set up right," Tim replied.

Matt helped Drew connect the power and run an ethernet cable into the device. There wasn't much else he could do to help her, so he sat back against the wall on the opposite side of the small room and watched her work. After an hour, Mike stopped by the room to check in.

"Security is set, and Eli just got the HF set up. We're all good," he said. "How's it going in here?"

"Well, she's hard at work. At least that's what I think the mumbled curses mean. I, on the other hand, am doing a fantastic job holding this wall up," Matt replied.

"Yes!" Drew exclaimed, pumping her fist. "I've got a connection."

Matt and Mike rushed over to look at her screen.

"I mean, there's not a lot to look at. It's just a command prompt, but I've got a connection with the system."

"Can I signal Frank and tell him we're set whenever he is?" Mike asked.

"Oh, no, sorry. We're not there yet," Drew said. "The connection is live. Now I have to bring the inject script and the generative-AI package online. Maybe another thirty minutes or so."

"Shouldn't we be getting fans or coolers or something?" Mike asked.

"It might eventually get hot, but what we are asking it to do is such a tiny fraction of what it was doing before, it almost doesn't even matter," Drew replied. "But if you find a fan, I'll still take it."

"I'll see what we can dig up," Mike said as he walked out of the room.

Drew turned her attention back to her computer and continued working. Matt resumed his position against the wall. He pulled out his notebook and started making notes about how they were going to make this work.

"OK, I think I'm ready for our first inject," Drew told Matt without looking up from her screen.

"All right. Is there anything we need to tweak the script we wrote yesterday?" Matt asked without getting up.

"No, I don't think so. The problem is that we won't actually know if it's worked or not until we get feedback from Frank's team," Drew said.

"Patience has never been one of my strong suits. Send it, and I'll let Mike know," Matt said as he walked out of the room and down the hall.

"Done," Drew called after him.

Matt walked into the control room, where Mike was talking with Mac and Sergeant Van. "We just sent the inject. Let Frank know that he should expect some company."

"Got it," Mike said. "While we're waiting for word back, we might as well start coming up with more ways to mess up their program."

"I'm one step ahead of you."

Chapter 18

Frank passed the hand mic back to Don. "We're on," he said to Lieutenant Nguyen and Rizzo. "They sent the inject, so with any luck we should start seeing some movement before too long. How's the obstruction looking?"

"Five healthy trees are completely blocking the road right at the end of the valley," Rizzo said. "No one is going to get over or around it without a lot of effort. We've got everything set to block the other end as well. What are the chances that this is actually going to work?"

"No idea," Frank said. "But if it does, then it's game on. Don, the LT, and I have spent the better part of an hour pre-coordinating fires, so we have everything dialed in. Now we wait."

From their concealed position two-thirds of the way up the side of the ridge, the team had an unobstructed view of the road that cut through the valley and snaked its way off to the north. Lieutenant Nguyen emplaced an observation post a kilometer further north, giving them early warning of any enemy movement. After checking on their soldiers one last time, Frank and Lieutenant Nguyen crawled into their positions and settled in for the long wait.

As time dragged on, Frank's mind drifted back to Kathy and

Kyra. She hadn't answered when he'd tried calling on the day of the invasion, so it had been nearly two weeks since he'd spoken with Kathy, and even longer since he had been able to FaceTime with Kyra. Now, lying between two fallen logs, he struggled to think about how life continued back at home without him and how many things he was missing in Kyra's life. He thought back to how much his father had been gone while Frank was growing up, wondering if Sam Gonzales had struggled with the distance as well.

"Movement," Lieutenant Nguyen said.

Looking down at his watch, Frank saw that he had been asleep for almost an hour. "What do you see?"

"Just there. Coming around that corner looks like a cargo truck. Possibly a gun truck in front of it."

"Let's pass the word and make sure everyone is ready," Frank said. As Lieutenant Nguyen passed word down the line, Frank checked in on the HF radio with the American advise-and-assist team that was working with the missile battery. Slowly, the convoy crawled into view along the river, cutting through the valley. Frank stopped counting after fifty.

"Is this too many for us?" Lieutenant Nguyen asked, voicing the same concern that had crept into Frank's mind.

"We can do this. Even if some do survive, they'll have a hell of a time getting to us up here," he replied.

The lead vehicle in the convoy drove all the way up to the trees obstructing the road. A Chinese soldier got out of the passenger seat to see how bad the blockage was while the rest of the convoy rolled to a stop, almost bumper to bumper. Slowly, the entire valley below them filled with vehicles.

Turning to his engineer, Frank motioned toward the back of the convoy. "Tyler, they are out past our explosives. I'm going to fire the northernmost target reference point, and I want you to set off your charge right after the initial salvo impacts."

The engineer nodded.

"Bootleg 2-1, this is Raven 1-6," Frank said into the radio. "Execute fire mission. TRPs AC four-zero-zero-one through AC four-zero-zero-six."

Several of the drivers had stepped out of their vehicles to smoke cigarettes while they waited for someone to clear the obstruction. Frank saw one take a long pull from a flask as the air rushed with the sound of incoming missiles. The entire valley erupted into flames. Although they were safely up on the ridge, the sheer ferocity of the incoming salvo forced the entire team onto the earth. Frank couldn't hear himself think through the deafening explosions that shook the valley. Just as suddenly as it had started, the barrage ended, leaving the road completely blanketed in smoke. The steady wind helped the smoke clear enough after a minute for Frank to start assessing the situation. Every vehicle in the convoy was destroyed, and he saw no signs of enemy movement.

"Bootleg 2-1, this is Raven 1-6. Fire mission complete. Estimate six-zero vehicles destroyed. Will confirm final battle damage assessment."

Turning to Lieutenant Nguyen, he nodded. "Let's go down and see what's happened."

Lieutenant Nguyen got his soldiers up and moving cautiously down the hillside. Once onto the road, they cleared through the objective in small teams, checking for any Chinese soldiers who had survived the initial attack and had any fight left in them. Although the dust had settled from the incoming missiles, several of the vehicles, including several fuel tankers, were still engulfed in flames, pouring acrid smoke into the air.

After a few tense minutes of waiting, all of the teams reported in to Lieutenant Nguyen that the area was secure.

"All right, let's have them go back through and gather whatever intel we can find. Let's get some firm numbers, unit identifications, and documents. That sort of thing. Nothing too big, though, because we're still going to have to walk it out of here. Let's be out of here in ten minutes."

Frank walked to a gun truck close to the center of the formation. The engine compartment was completely gone, and there were several gaping holes in the crew compartment where shrapnel had torn through. Inside, the bodies of four Chinese soldiers sat motionless. Frank checked their pockets, starting with the front passenger and working his way around. He collected cell phones and a notebook and put them into his bag. Looking up and down the column, he saw the soldiers searching through what little remained. At the nine-minute mark, Lieutenant Nguyen ordered them all off of the objective. In two more minutes, the team disappeared back into the jungle, leaving the burning remains of the convoy behind.

-

"Frank says it was total destruction of over seventy vehicles," Mike said. "There were a lot of fuelers too, which helped out with the size of the explosions when they went up. I wasn't sure if we were going to pull this off, but your trick worked."

"I'd like to say that I knew it would all along, but to be honest, I'm pretty shocked myself," Drew admitted. "Since it's coming from a known source, our little device here, the system simply trusts the data and treats it like every other piece of information coming in. In this case, I just had the system generate multiple reports that their primary western supply route was out, and recommended an alternate that went right through the valley you all specified."

"Well, it just paid off in a big way," Matt added, "and now it's time to kick our plan into gear."

"I've got something else to help with that," Drew said, handing Mike a cell phone. "You've been relying on your high-frequency radios as your only method of communication, since we're reasonably sure that the Chinese forces can't detect or intercept their signals. While we were waiting to hear back from Frank, I wrote an app that will allow us to talk to the other team in real time without Eli having to mess around with radios. I've set it up so that whatever messages we send are routed through our device here. We then hide it as something other than what it actually is. Any AI sifting through the data should discount our traffic as noise."

"You did that in a few hours?" Matt asked in disbelief.

Drew shrugged. "It really wasn't that hard. I started with an open-source chat application and then used our system here to help me write the rest of the code. AI code assist has made programming so much easier."

"Still, that's amazing," Matt said.

"OK," Mike said, "but how do we get this out to the Vietnamese army so they can start talking securely?"

"I wouldn't do that," Matt interjected before Drew could speak. "We can get away with an anomaly if it actually is an anomaly, but if they see thousands and thousands of anomalies as use picks up, they're sure to figure this out. Even more so when it correlates with a sudden drop in other forms of communications traffic. I don't think we can have more than a couple people using this system without risking discovery."

"Five is the number I came up with when I ran the calculations," Drew offered. "We have to limit it to one here and four others. The fewer we have using it, the better we are. For now, though, I assume that you are going to want one or two with Frank and one with whoever you're coordinating through with your bosses."

"So how do we actually get them onto this system?" Mike asked. "We can't exactly bring them here."

"It's the twenty-first century. I published it to the App Store, so all they have to do is go download it," Drew said, handing Mike a piece of paper. "Here are four other usernames and passwords that they can use to log in once they have it. We'll need the information off of their phones to put into our system here, though."

"This is brilliant," Mike said. "I'll get Eli to pass it along. It's going to make things so much easier."

As Mike turned to leave, the three heard footsteps running down the hall. Tim burst into the room a moment later. "The team's under attack."

Running into the control room, they could hear Eli talking on the radio.

"I copy, Frank: No casualties in the initial exchange. You're in a small farmhouse eight hundred meters west of your vehicle-staging point with good cover. You estimate the enemy as a squad composed of six to nine Veiled Dragon robots."

"Oh, shit," Matt said. "That's not good. Mike, can we pinpoint which building they're in so we can call in some artillery to help them out?"

"I already passed their location to the artillery guys. They're retasking a UAV, but it won't be overhead for fifteen minutes. Nothing else is in range."

"They'll be dead by then," Mike said.

"You said the enemy is robots? Were there any soldiers with them?" Matt asked.

"He didn't say anything about soldiers. Let me clarify," Eli said, relaying the question over the radio. "No humans. Just the robots."

"I've got an idea," Matt replied.

-

Frank pressed the headset against his head, attempting to block the deafening sound of machine-gun fire echoing off the concrete walls. "He wants me to do what? Play on my phone in the middle of a firefight?" Frank asked. Looking around the room, he saw Lieutenant Nguyen moving from position to position, checking on his soldiers. They were holding their own for now, but that wouldn't last. Especially against a drone force.

Unzipping the utility pouch on his kit, he pulled out his phone and powered it on. "OK, walk me through this." Frank followed the instructions Eli relayed to him.

Alright, I'm in. now what? He typed into Drew's messenger app.

Perfect! Now, I want you to send a regular text message to Mike's number. It's off, so he won't get it, but that's not the point. "Radio hit, down to cell phone in my comms plan. Four remaining including Lieutenant Nguyen. Found way back out of farm house. Going to make a run for it. Send in artillery on our position when available to destroy enemy force."

Frank sent the message and stared at the phone, waiting for a response. A minute later, his phone vibrated.

I see your message, and it's been flagged in the system. Now the hard part: have the entire unit stop shooting. Play dead.

Frank relayed the order to Lieutenant Nguyen, who gave him a puzzled look, but immediately issued it down to his soldiers. Thirty seconds later, the firing inside the small building stopped.

Done, Frank typed. *This better work.*

Although the cacophony of rifle and machine gun fire had ceased, the sound of incoming rounds impacting the building increased to fill the void, building to such an intensity that Frank wasn't sure that the structure wasn't about to collapse in on itself. His mind went to Kathy and Kyra, how much he wished he could see them one more time, and then to the wives and children of every other man there. *At least,* he thought, *we're going out fighting for something good.*

As soon as he finished that thought, the incoming fire stopped all at once.

"Stay down," Frank said. "Keep everyone down and out of view, but make sure the machine-gun team at the door is ready in case they make their move."

Frank could hear movement outside the building and the sound of treads rolling past and slowly dissipating into the distance. Soon, the team was left lying in silence.

They've broken off their attack. It sounds like they've moved west.
Good. You shouldn't run into them if you head southeast.
What did you do?
Less talking, more running. Explain later.

As quickly as he could without making noise, he got the team up and moving. Ten minutes later, they had reached their vehicle-staging point and set off down the dirt road that would bring them back across the front line. Frank heard an explosion behind him, and turned to see a plume of smoke rising from where they had just been. His phone vibrated.

You and the entire ODA have just been killed calling in a missile strike on your own position. My condolences.

-

"I feel like we just got struck by lightning twice in the same day. There's no way that should have worked," Mike said.

"Why wouldn't it have worked, though?" Drew asked. "They received updated intelligence that the team of American and Vietnamese soldiers they were planning to attack had left. Then they started receiving intelligence that said those soldiers were moving off to the west, based off of where their cell phones were located. Pair those two reports coming from a reliable source with the unit on the ground noticing they were no longer meeting resistance. What conclusion would you draw?"

"That they had somehow gotten past me and were currently escaping," Mike admitted. "And then I would stop shooting at nothing and try to chase them down."

"Exactly, so all we had to do was put together some data that would logically lead to that conclusion, which the AI did without questioning it since it was coming from trusted sources," Drew said.

"How did you make it look like they were running away in a specific direction?" Mike asked.

"I gave it some fake positions from their phones that set them moving off to the west."

"It's interesting to me that the squad was made entirely of Veiled Dragon robots. I thought that they were supposed to be integrated units," Matt said.

"That's what we saw during our first encounter with them on the bridge," Mike added.

"Right," Matt said. "I remember a press conference where some Chinese general was proudly heralding in a new era where men and machines would fight alongside each other. But that's not what we saw here. There didn't seem to be any humans around. If the opposite were true—all humans—I could see that, since there are much fewer dragons and not all of the units would have them. To have all dragons, though, seems a break from their initial plan. Why would they do that?" Matt asked.

"Maybe they didn't," Drew offered.

"What do you mean?"

"What if that wasn't a choice made by humans. If the AI is truly running the show, then it could have made that change," she said.

"Can it do that?"

"When I first got to DARPA, they were training the system based on historical data. It was part training, and part seeing how it would have done things differently. I showed up when they were running it through some battles from the First World War. I don't really know much about military history, but Rich kept going on and on about how the AI had started playing out the battles very differently, and that one of the things it kept doing was rearranging how it had pooled its different types of units."

"So it changed the way it task-organized?" Mike clarified.

"That may have been the term he used; I don't know. But when it did that, it started winning more."

"Well, that's not good for us here," Mike said.

"It wasn't good for the simulated soldiers, either," Drew said. "We were all horrified at how it was getting its results. It essentially created units that it didn't care about at all and sent them in to be slaughtered. It did that to save its best units and put them in a better position to win."

"Because World War I wasn't horrifying enough," Mike said.

"Again, I don't know history that well, but it did apparently win much sooner than the real war. Do you think that's what it's doing here?"

"I have no idea," Matt admitted, "but if it is, that's something we can use. Eli, were you able to get the Joint Task Force headquarters up on DrewNet?"

"They're up," Eli responded.

"DrewNet?" Drew asked, "Please kill me now if that's what we're calling it."

"Then come up with a better name," Matt smiled. "Eli, can you ask them for reports on enemy-force disposition and composition? Specifically, we're looking for instances of homogenous units—only humans or only dragons."

"Got it. I'll see what they say," Eli said.

"What's your plan?" Mike asked.

"We know that it has seen success adopting a strategy of rearranging its forces and sacrificing its low-quality units," Matt said. "We've also just seen evidence that it may be testing dragon-pure units to see how they fare. In this case, a squad of at most nine dragons just wiped out an entire American ODA and a Vietnamese Ranger platoon. That sounds like a pretty big success. What if we feed into that notion to get it to adopt that strategy across its entire force?"

"We're going to show it the winning strategy?" Mike asked.

"It's not really a winning strategy, though. Sure, it worked in the simulation Drew's team ran, but that didn't involve actual humans. Imagine you're a commander. You've been told that you now have drones that can help do the fighting for you and take away some of the danger to your forces. They can do the more dangerous tasks, allowing you to preserve your combat power and keep more of your soldiers alive. Then, as the fighting intensifies, your drones are removed and put into separate units. You might think to yourself, *This is great. Now those units can be sent to the most dangerous areas.* Instead of that, however, your unit is sent into the worst of the fighting, and you start to take heavier and heavier casualties. How does that make you feel?"

"I'd be pretty pissed," Mike admitted.

"Hell yeah, you'd be pissed! Your soldiers would be too, because they are humans with individual thoughts and emotions and a strong desire to live. They aren't just going to accept their new status as cannon fodder."

"So we're going to take advantage of the man-versus-machine division the AI creates and turn them against each other? That could take a long time. Much longer than this country has. Hanoi could fall in a matter of days."

"If it happened naturally. But we can help it along thanks to our device. We can feed information into the system and drive a wedge straight into the heart of the Chinese military."

"How do we do that?" Drew asked.

"First, we have to get JTF and the Vietnamese on board. They're going to have to do the heavy lifting on this one," Matt said. "While I'm working on that, Drew, can you get a voice function added into DrewNet?"

"Only if you promise to never say 'DrewNet' again."

Chapter 19

Frank looked around the room as Lieutenant Nguyen finished his pitch. The highest-ranking members of the Ministry of Defense sat in silence. Finally, the minister spoke.

"If I am hearing you correctly, you are asking us to allow their strongest forces the opportunity to gain more momentum. To give them free passage and expose our very hearts to the daggers of the enemy. And we are just supposed to trust that you have some secret knowledge of what the enemy will do and some capability to whisper words into their ears that will somehow turn them against each other. Is that what you are asking?"

"Not free passage, Minister," Lieutenant Nguyen said. "But I am asking for your trust."

"We must fight them. Like we did the last time they tried this foolishness."

"Minister, we will lose that fight," Lieutenant Nguyen replied. "Do not be misled by our last engagement with the Chinese. Instead, look at what we accomplished against the French and the Americans. We accepted our adversaries' strengths and our weaknesses. We chose our strategy to suit our reality, not what we wished it to be. This dagger will certainly pierce our heart if we do not take away the enemy's strength to drive the blade home. You have read the reports from the front. You know this is the truth we must accept. Captain Gonzales's plan is our chance, and we must be bold enough to grasp this victory from an otherwise certain defeat."

Defense Minister Lam rose from his chair and walked to the window, staring out into the hills sloping up from the relocated headquarters. "Our current path leads to defeat," he said without turning from the window. "We can pretend this is not the case, but the facts are irrefutable. Even if the aid promised from our allies arrived tomorrow, it would not be enough to turn the tide. I do not know if you can deliver on what you have said, but I am willing to grant you a short window to try. In the meantime, General Giang, please prepare alternative solutions for the continued defense and transition into a protracted resistance."

With that, the defense minister left the room.

Frank stood and slipped his notebook into his pocket. As he walked to the door with Lieutenant Nguyen, he was stopped by the only other American in the room.

"Does Washington know what you're up to?" Brigadier General Miles asked. As the commander of the joint task force responsible for advising and assisting the Vietnamese military, he was technically Frank's superior, although the two had not met.

"Sir, Admiral Jennings is aware of our plan."

"Your idiot plan. You're going to get a lot of people killed. Didn't you read about what happened in Ukraine? It wasn't parlor tricks that helped the Ukrainian military. It was steel— the tanks and artillery we poured into the country to help them fight off the Russian incursion."

"Sir, with all due respect, that steel isn't here yet. Until it arrives, the Vietnamese are on their own, and this is the best chance that they have. Until I am told to shut down by SOCPAC, I will continue doing everything in my power to help our allies."

"Don't get too comfortable, Captain. That order is imminent," General Miles said as he turned and walked out of the conference room.

"I do not think you have made a friend in the general," Lieutenant Nguyen said, walking down the sidewalk next to Frank.

"I think you're right about that. Unfortunately, as the JTF commander he'll have a lot of sway. Especially once more aid starts to pour in. If we are going to pull this off, we're going to have to show some results quickly."

-

"I still don't understand why we have to do this," Don Ramsey said, stepping down from the cab of a gray box truck. "I mean, Chief's team can just inject whatever reports we want through their device."

Frank rolled up the door to the cargo area and hopped inside. "Think about it. What happens if you're receiving reports that tell you one thing, but then you keep having your frontline elements reporting things that are totally different. Sure, that'll happen from time to time with the fog of war, but eventually they are going to wonder what's up."

The two men grabbed the handles of one of the body bags and passed it to a pair of Rangers waiting at the ramp.

"If there are supposed to be as many or more troops in this area as in the sector to our west, then units rolling through here need to be finding at least some of their bodies," Frank continued. "Plus, it gives a chance to plant more physical intelligence artifacts that give credence to the story we're feeding it."

After the ten bags were unloaded, Frank and Don hopped down from the cargo area and picked their way through the debris that had fallen onto the street from where a rocket had struck a small apartment building the day before. Inside, the Rangers were at work positioning the bodies in the room that had been struck. Fortunately, no one had been injured in that strike, but after a few minutes, the team had staged the area to look as if an entire platoon might have been wiped out in the attack.

"All right, that should be good enough," Frank said. "Based on their current rate of advancement, the lead element of drones should pass through here sometime in the morning. We'd best be long gone before then."

The sergeant made one more sweep around the room to check that everything was in position, and then headed back down to the truck.

Package 1 delivered and staged. Returning to base now. ETA: two hours, he typed.

Received. Packages 2 and 3 also in position.

Don left fifty meters between the cargo truck and the lead vehicle as they drove back south away from the front. Frank could see the driver of the sedan doing his best to retrace the exact path they took on the way in. After the last driver had hit a mine the day before that had thrown his truck's engine fifty yards down the road, Frank couldn't really blame the new driver for being cautious. They were lucky that only the driver had been injured in that blast, and the new driver seemed to be doing everything he could to not follow suit.

Two hours later, they pulled through the gate of their team house and parked next to the other cargo truck. Shutting down the engine, Don looked at Frank.

"I'm going to need to take a scouring pad with me into the shower. I'm not sure a simple washcloth is going to clean any of what we just did off me," he said.

"Aren't you the one who told me that you were ready to, quote, 'stack some bodies' when you heard about the Chinese invasion?" Frank shot back.

"Sir, this is definitely not what I had in mind," Don said, sliding down from the driver's seat.

The pair grabbed their gear from the cab and laid it out in the foyer of the house next to the gear from Rizzo's team. Walking into the kitchen, they ran into Rizzo, who handed them a beer.

"Glad you two finally made it," Rizzo said. "I was trying to work out how to explain to Kathy how you died. I'm not sure that it would make sense to anyone outside of this room here."

"I'll keep that in mind when I choose the time and place of my death," Frank said.

"As always, thank you for your service. We've got a meeting with Mike and Matt in ten minutes if you want to get cleaned up beforehand."

"That I do. I'll be back in a bit."

After a quick shower and change of clothes, Frank was seated next to Rizzo in the living room when his phone vibrated.

How'd everything go tonight? —Mike

Everything went according to plan. All three sites were staged, no contact, no issues. —Frank

Glad to hear it. —Mike

Have we gotten any intel back on effects yet? —Frank

It's only been a couple days, so we aren't seeing anything drastic, but here's what we know so far. There is definitely evidence that the Chinese have reorganized themselves segregating the dragons into their own units. No reports in the last two days have humans and dragons operating together at all. They are only seen separate from each other. If that is the case and the AI is adopting a tactic the DARPA engineers have seen before, then the next move for it would be to preserve its preferred units, sacrificing other units in an attempt to tie up as many of our forces as possible. Although fighting in the central corridor has increased in intensity and there are indications that additional Chinese forces have moved into the area, we aren't sure that this is because the AI has adopted this strategy. —Mike

What about any reflections of fracturing within the chain of command? —Frank

There is some SIGINT that suggests that several of the ground commanders are displeased at how the battle is unfolding and several have made specific reference to being commanded by a machine, but nothing that would indicate they are ready to revolt. This is corroborated by a pair of recently captured Chinese officers. —Mike

So best we can tell is that our plan is likely working, but we don't know for sure. Nor do we know how long it would take. —Frank

Correct. We're getting everything secondhand from the JTF intel cell and from the Vietnamese intel folks. They're the only other ones on DNet, though, so our view is limited here. Drew added a message board to the DNet app, so you can read through the reports they attached when you have time. —Mike

What's the next plan? I'm not sure that adding more bodies for the eastern corridor is going to be the ticket. —Frank

The commander in the central corridor is going to launch a

significant counteroffensive in the morning. We've already pre-staged a tranche of injects to go out when he does that should add some confusion to help the Vietnamese and advance some of the friction within the Chinese command. —Mike

Got it. We'll head out there in a few hours and link up with the commander to lend a hand. Have there been any issues up there with you? —Frank

So far so good. We are all going a little stir crazy in this building, but we're doing well. Going to have to make a resupply run soon. Sorry I'm missing all the fun. Stay safe out there. —Mike

Frank closed the app and put the phone in his pocket. "Man, it's really hard to know if we're on the right track or just making a bunch of worthless busywork for ourselves," he said to Rizzo.

"I know what you mean, but you can't fight the war. Not your place. Until that aid package gets here, confusing and sowing dissent into the Chinese war machine is about the best we can do," Rizzo replied.

"I hope you're right. I'm going to go try to get a couple hours of sleep before we roll out. Let me know if anything interesting kicks off."

Chapter 20

"Any news from Frank?" Matt asked, sitting down in an empty chair next to Mike in the control room.

"He checked in a few minutes ago while you were in with Drew. The first day of the counteroffensive seems to have gone surprisingly well. The Chinese are putting up a fight, but so far, the Vietnamese have been making some progress. They weren't sure if the Chinese were just caught off guard, or what the deal was. They definitely didn't expect to have to deal with the number of soldiers the Vietnamese have thrown at them, and it's causing them to have to readjust."

"How so?" Matt asked.

"They've slowed down in the east. Despite the gains that they had been making there, they really haven't pushed much since we started. The JTF's assessment is that they are having to reallocate resources from the east into the central corridor to bolster their defense. In turn, the Vietnamese Fourth Division is also being moved into the area," Mike said.

"Popular place to be, I suppose."

"If you're a human. Our theory about segregating units seems to be true. There haven't been any reports of encountering dragons anywhere but in the east. Seems like they are content to fight it out twentieth-century style."

"If our theory is actually correct, then they are planning on doing something with those units," Matt said. "Maybe they're lulling us into a false sense of security on the east in an effort to get us to shift forces out of the area. Probably worth floating that idea up to JTF just in case. They can run their analysis and see what they want to do about it."

"Good point. I suppose it's wishful thinking that we just have them on the back foot," Mike said.

"Mention it to Frank, too, the next time you talk to him, so it's in his mind. Maybe he'll see something out there that can tell us what they're up to."

"You might be able to tell him in person tomorrow. If they can maintain their current pace, we're likely to be on the Vietnamese side of the line before too long."

"Have we come up with a plan for that?" Matt asked. "Seems like we are at risk of encountering some retreating Chinese or some advancing Vietnamese forces as the front moves past us."

"I think our best bet for the Chinese is to make this building a pain in the ass to try to get into," Mike said. "It doesn't have any tactical value, so there's not an actual reason to occupy it. It would just be a target of opportunity for soldiers to see if there's anything of value they can steal on their way through. That person isn't going to work very hard to get into a place like this."

"I'd buy that line of thinking."

"For the Vietnamese, it's kind of the same thing. We've passed up our position to the JTF, and they have assured us that the Vietnamese command is tracking. As long as we can keep the casuals away, we should be good."

"I hope you're right," Matt said. "Do you need anything from me?"

"Nah, I think we're good."

Matt got up and walked out of the control room and back down the hall. Drew had fully staked her claim to the transmission closet and had made it as comfortable as possible. He had found himself spending most of his time in there helping her generate prompts to feed into the AI's system. At first, it was a slow, deliberate process to craft each inject, but the more they used the system the better it got at producing the sorts of intelligence reports and data that they were looking for. Now, they had to create the general theme of what they wanted to get into the system and the device would take care of everything else.

"What's cookin'?" he said walking into the room.

"Good lookin'," Drew replied absently. A moment later, she shook her head as her mind caught up with what she had just said. She swiveled around in her chair to face the door, visibly flustered. "Anyhoo, I think I've just about finished up with the last of the injects if you want to check them over before we send them off."

"Sure," Matt said.

Drew stood up and moved out of the way so Matt could sit down, but hovered behind him so she could read over his shoulder. Matt sat and scrolled through the files. Troop movements, casualty estimates, intercepted voice communications, requests for eight million rolls of toilet paper. That last one made him laugh out loud.

"You like that one, don't you?" Drew smiled. "Either someone is going to get chewed out for messing up a supply request so badly, or they are about to be the recipients of enough TP to supply the entire army for a year. Either way, someone ain't going to be happy."

"If it works, a lot of somebodies aren't going to be happy, because no one else in southern China will be able to get their hands on any. Like when people started hoarding it during the COVID outbreak."

"That was my source of inspiration, actually. I was pretty young, but I vividly remember how upset my mom was."

"Drew Drum: evil genius."

Drew curtsied.

"These are great. Launch them. From what Mike tells me, things are going smoothly with the counteroffensive. We might actually be in Vietnamese-controlled territory tomorrow," Matt said, relinquishing the seat to Drew.

"Wouldn't that be something. Maybe then we could go outside. I've forgotten what the sun looks like. Does it even still exist?"

"Don't be dramatic. Plus, you're a computer nerd. I thought you were allergic to sunlight," Matt poked.

"Ouch. I'd be mad if that weren't so accurate. I'm not sure how to feel—seen? Attacked?"

"Confused is how I like my women. Or at least that's how I'm told I make them feel."

"Oh, so I'm one of those women you like then?"

"You . . . never mind. It's late, and I'm going to bed before I stick my foot further in my mouth."

Matt walked out the room and flopped down on his bag in the hallway.

"A wise choice," Drew called after him.

"You know, it doesn't have the same effect when you leave a room dramatically but sleep right outside the door."

"It really doesn't," Drew agreed.

Matt smiled and pulled his poncho liner over his head.

-

The building shook, knocking off bits of plaster from the ceiling that rained down on Matt, jolting him awake.

"Drew, are you OK?" he shouted. He threw off his poncho liner, sending plaster flying across the hallway, and rushed into the transmission closet.

"What the hell was that?" Drew answered.

"I don't know, but whatever it was isn't good. Let's go check in with Mike," Matt said, not waiting for her to reply.

"Mike, were we hit?" Matt asked as he jogged into the control room with his kit slung over his shoulder.

Right behind him, Tim rushed in the room in a full panic. "We have to get out of here right now. Someone just blew a big hole in the dam, and I don't think it's going to hold much longer."

"Oh shit," Matt said.

Another explosion shook the building. The lights flickered and cut out, sending the room into total darkness. Mike switched on the small flashlight he kept in his pocket.

"Everybody out. If the dam is going to go, we need to get to high ground right now," he shouted, lighting the way to the front door. Matt got there first. When he opened it, sunlight flooded into the hallway, temporarily blinding him but signaling the way out for the rest of the team.

Once outside, Matt burst into a run with Drew close on his heels. "There!" he shouted, pointing to the top of the hill that overlooked the dam's control building.

Doing her best to keep up with Matt, Drew turned her head

to look over at the dam. There was a large hole missing from the top of the dam with water rushing through. Farther down the face, she saw a crater where a missile had struck almost dead center. She watched in horror as cracks splintered out from the impact site, sending chunks of concrete into the river below.

A third explosion erupted in the same place as the existing crater, knocking the team to the ground. The force of this explosion accelerated the speed at which the cracks spread, and soon the entire structure began to break up.

Matt grabbed Drew, pulling her up to her feet and back into a run. He could see her shouting something but couldn't hear what she was saying over the roar of water now forcing its way past the crumbling remnants of the dam. As they continued running, water started flooding in. At first, it was enough to splash with each of their footsteps, but every few steps he could tell a noticeable difference in the depth. Looking up toward the hill, Matt wasn't sure if they were going to make it there before the water swept them away.

Their pace slowed as they had to fight for each step against the current, which had risen to knee level. Drew lost her footing, and Matt tightened his grip on her hand, bracing against the rising water so she could get her feet back under her. Behind them, several of the Rangers also lost their battle against the rushing water and were swept away. Matt watched as Tim turned around and pushed through the water back toward two more scrambling men. They tried and failed to regain control, pulled downstream just before he could reach them. Tim slapped the water and reversed course but tripped and disappeared under the water. Matt looked for the Green Beret to reemerge, but to no avail.

"Keep going. We can make it," he shouted to Drew, although he was becoming less sure they would make it to the relative safety of the high ground before the water grew too strong.

Fifty feet away, the ground turned sharply uphill. If they could just make it to that spot, Matt thought, they could escape the flood as the massive reservoir drained into the valley below. Sensing movement out of the corner of his eye, he turned to see a massive tree, uprooted by the flood and heading right for them. He pulled Drew into him and braced as the branches struck and dragged them down into the current.

The tangle of limbs and branches pushed the two underwater as the tree rolled over them in the water. After it had passed, Matt pulled his head up above the water and fought to regain control. Twice, he tried to put his feet down, but he was moving too fast. Accepting the fact that they were being swept away, Matt turned downstream and looked for another way out.

"Hold on to me," he said. Flipping onto his stomach, he put Drew's hand on the back of his belt. Once he felt her grip harden, he released her hand and started swimming toward the edge of the swelling river. They were pushed under several more times by the turbulent water, but Matt slowly made it to the side. Looking downstream, he saw a tree at the water's edge that had a chain wrapped around its base.

Reaching out, he grabbed onto the chain and braced as it swung them around. The chain slid in his hand, tearing a hole in his palm from the sudden deceleration.

"Climb over me and pull yourself up onto the bank," he ordered. Drew struggled but managed to work her way up over his back and onto land. Once there, she reached out her hand. Matt grabbed it, and Drew pulled with every ounce of strength she had.

"Keep going! We made it out, but still need to get a lot higher," Matt said, rising back to his feet. Free from the force of the water, they quickly put distance between them and the now-raging river as they climbed to the top of the hill. Reaching the summit, the two collapsed onto the ground, panting. Matt looked out and saw that the hill they were on was higher than the level of the reservoir, so they were out of immediate danger of being engulfed again.

"Do you see anyone else?" Drew asked between gasps.

"No. I saw some of the Rangers swept away, but I don't know where anyone is."

"How did they find us? We were so careful."

"That wasn't aimed at us. Someone just took out the dam on purpose," Matt answered. "The first missile might have just missed us if we were the target, but all three missiles hit the dam itself. The third one was also delayed enough that it was likely sent in after they saw the structure still intact. No, that wasn't at us."

"Oh God, all the people." Drew said with a look of horror on her face. "There's no telling how many people live below here."

"Thousands. Tens of thousands. Plus any soldiers that were in the . . ." Matt stopped midsentence and pulled out his phone. Looking at the screen, he saw that it was no longer functioning from being submerged.

"What?" Drew asked.

"Directly downstream from here is the frontline trace for the central corridor. All those soldiers are in the path of this flood barreling towards them. And Frank's team is somewhere in there too."

Drew stared at him, unable to find any words.

"We can't think about that right now. You and I may be out of the flood path, but we're still not out of danger. This area is still on the Chinese side of the line, and we're alone and exposed. We need to find a way to get out of here." Matt took the knife out of his pocket and stripped off his button-down shirt, revealing a soaked gray T-shirt underneath. Cutting a strip of cloth from the bottom, he wrapped his hand.

Drew sat with her head resting on her knees. Doing her best to compose herself, she lifted her head and looked at Matt. "Thank you," she said. "You saved my life. Again."

"You're welcome. Can you move?"

"Yeah, I'm OK," she answered softly.

Skirting the top of the ridge, Matt and Drew slowly made their way south. Every few minutes, Matt paused to listen for any movement that might indicate enemy troops in the area. Once satisfied they weren't about to run into a patrol, they continued on their way. In the late afternoon, they came across a small house nestled into the side of the hill. With no signs of people around, Matt and Drew went inside to see if they could find water and something to eat. Searching the kitchen, they found several bottles of water, drank two immediately, and put two more into a cloth bag Drew found draped across a chair. Although there were several bags of rice, the only food they could eat without taking time to prepare it was a couple candy bars. Filling up the water bottles from the sink, they each took a candy bar and ate it before setting off once again.

As the sun set, they reached the outskirts of a village and hid in an overgrown irrigation ditch until night fell. Once darkness had fully consumed them, they picked their way along an alley to a parked car. Jimmying the lock, Matt slipped inside and unlocked the passenger side so that Drew could get in. She had barely settled in when the engine roared to life.

"Steal a lot of cars, do we?" Drew asked, raising an eyebrow.

"Just lucky, I guess." Matt smiled as he put the car in gear. Keeping the headlights off, he slowly made his way through the village and onto the road south, toward Hanoi.

Chapter 21

Matt clipped the visitor's badge to his shirt and thanked the security guard before turning to follow a sergeant who looked as if she hadn't slept in a week.

"Sorry for the delay, sir," she said, trying her best to cover her weariness. "Your credentials didn't come up in the usual system, so I had to confirm who you were with General Miles's aide."

"That happens sometimes," Matt offered. "Databases don't seem to like me for some reason. How's everything going here?"

"We're still fully engaged with support to their defenses, but we've shifted a lot of our assets to help with rescue efforts. It's a real mess. Can you imagine what that would have been like for those people who got caught in the flood's path?"

"No," Matt lied, "it must have been terrifying for them."

"These people really have been through so much. Anyways, here's the conference room, sir. The briefing will start in a couple minutes when General Miles is done with an office call."

"Thank you. Get some sleep," Matt said to the sergeant who smiled as she turned and walked back toward the entrance. He stepped into the back of the conference room and slid into an empty seat against the wall. The room was filled with a mixture of uniforms from the various coalition partners that made up the joint task force, and Matt looked around for any familiar faces. Finding none, he sat back and waited for the general.

"JTF commander," an authoritative voice called, bringing everyone in the room to their feet.

"Carry on. Sit down. How are we doing this morning?" General Miles said.

Taking his cue, a colonel stood and began talking. "Good morning, sir. Early this morning, we received reports that Chinese forces from the eastern corridor had withdrawn, and we confirmed this movement through aerial ISR." The colonel progressed the slide to show overhead imagery depicting a column of dragons moving north along one of the main roads. "Despite initial indications that they were exploiting the widespread flooding, it seems that this is no longer the case. The autonomous division now appears to be retreating towards the border, joining the rest of the Chinese army in a full-scale withdrawal."

"Are there any Chinese units still in the fight?" General Miles asked.

"No, sir, not that we have found. They seem to be reeling from the destruction of the dam just as much as we are. President Zhao Qi released a statement this morning noting the incredible tragedy of the situation, promising that the Chinese government would not interfere with rescue efforts, and claiming a desire to negotiate with the Vietnamese government for the return of their citizens killed in the disaster."

"That's an odd change of tune when they're the ones that blew up the thing to begin with," the general commented.

"Yes sir," the colonel agreed. "We are still trying to figure out what their move is here."

"My guess is that it's a trap. As soon as the Vietnamese army lets their guard down and goes all in on their recovery efforts, the Chinese will spring their trap and finish the job once and for all."

"That is possible, sir. We're calling in all sorts of assets to provide early warnings if the forces start maneuvering in any way that might turn offensive again."

"It'll come. Just give it a few days. We won't chase them out of the country, but my advice to the MOD is to follow closely behind and reestablish defensive positions along the way."

"I think that's prudent, sir," the colonel agreed. "Pending any questions, that's my update for today."

"Thanks, Milo," General Miles said, turning his attention back to the screen at the front of the room as it advanced to the next slide.

Matt stopped paying attention to the briefing as his mind wandered. It had been a little over twenty-four hours since he'd checked Drew and himself into a two-bedroom suite in the Intercontinental downtown. After sending their clothes out to the laundry and calling out for room service, Matt sat in the shower for half an hour trying to make sense of everything that had just happened. Overwhelmed by a wave of exhaustion, he had fallen into bed and was asleep before his head hit the pillow.

Despite sleeping for six hours and putting on his freshly washed clothes, Matt still felt weary. He hoped that the briefing would be short so that he could have the required conversation with General Miles before catching a flight back home. Eventually, he was jolted out of his own thoughts when everyone in the room stood up as the general walked out of the room. Matt got up and followed him.

"Sir," he said, closing the gap between them, "I'm Major Anderson. Is now still a good time?"

"Good morning, Major Anderson. It's never a good time, but this is as good as it is going to get. Walk with me."

Matt moved alongside the general as they continued down the long corridor.

"Tell me," the general said, "what's the status of your operation?"

"Sir, there is no more operation. Both the team at the dam and the one supporting the maneuver element were wiped out in the flood. Besides me, only one other person survived. All of our equipment is gone. Without it, there's no reason for us to remain in country."

"Well, that's something on which you and I agree, Major," General Miles said.

"Sir?"

"It's no secret that I was never a fan of what you were doing. I'm not even convinced that the destruction of the dam wasn't an accident born out of the Chinese effort to destroy you. Either way, I am glad I'm no longer forced to deal with whatever it was you were up to. Please give my condolences to your command for the loss of their soldiers. That was a tragedy," General Miles said in a genuine tone.

"Yes sir. I will."

"Farewell, Major Anderson," General Miles said, stepping out of the corridor into a small office.

Matt watched as the door closed behind the general, and then walked back out of the building the way he came.

-

"Matt, come in. I heard you were back in town," Colonel Banks said. "Have a seat."

"Thanks, sir. I got back in two days ago." Matt settled onto the blue couch that stretched along one of the walls in the colonel's office.

"How are you? I heard about the ODA you were with. I wish I could say something, but in my thirty years in the service I've yet to come up with anything that doesn't sound trite when we lose people. It never gets easier."

"Thanks, sir. I appreciate that." Matt looked at the floor for a moment. "Fortunately, the team's senior bravo, Tim Wells, ended up making it back a week later along with one of the Vietnamese Rangers. I'm going to be headed out to First Group next week for the memorial service."

"Thanks for doing that. It'll mean a lot to the team. I read all the reporting coming out about the incident. You and General Miles paint a very different picture with some equally different conclusions," Colonel Banks said, changing the subject.

"Isn't that the name of the game for us, sir? We just have a better vantage point for what's going on. Case in point: the JTF staff completely missed the supposed Chinese missile test shot that took out a huge facility south of Kunming. That wasn't a test shot. That was them finishing off what I think might be the first human-AI civil war."

"You may be right. If I'm reading your version correctly, their AI pulled out one of the tricks it learned in training— segregating the dragons from the humans, and then using the units it deemed inferior, the humans, as cannon fodder to manipulate its opponent. In this case, it drew the main

Vietnamese force into the central corridor and then blew up the dam to destroy that force even though it meant also killing tens of thousands of its own forces."

"Makes sense when it saw how many humans it had to spare back in mainland China. It would have worked too, if the military commanders hadn't minded being sent to the slaughter alongside their soldiers. Turns out, though, that they didn't appreciate this strategy and took out the AI in that missile strike to regain control of the military."

"I saw the China-internal reporting indicating that the officer corps sent an ultimatum to the party leadership threatening to turn against them if they didn't stop the war and reinstate human control over the military—minus the ones whose bright idea it was in the first place," Colonel Banks added.

"Couldn't have happened to a nicer bunch of people. Just too bad it had to come at the expense of so many Vietnamese lives."

"The international community is holding China to account for their actions, but it's going to take the Vietnamese people years to recover."

"What about our encryption problem?"

"I almost forgot that that's where this whole thing actually started," Colonel Banks admitted. "The super nerds at the NSA have been hard at work reverse engineering the device you brought to them. They've already figured out how to make their own, and are supposedly close to a new encryption algorithm that is hardened against quantum technology. Just don't ask me to explain it. Ten seconds in and my eyes glazed over."

"So the great game continues. Offense and defense locked in a timeless battle for supremacy."

"You're right about that. Speaking of the great game, when are you back to operational status? The ambassador to Chile won't stop bugging the SOUTHCOM commander about help with some problems with the Russians. I want to bring you in as project lead."

"Well, sir, I was planning on taking a week of leave, but I—"

"No, don't cancel those plans," Colonel Banks interrupted. "Chile has waited this long. Another week won't hurt them."

"Thanks. I'll check in once I get back." Matt stood up from the couch and headed to the door.

"Matt," Colonel Banks called after him. "Thanks. For everything. You did exactly what we needed and I expected from you."

"Thank you, sir. See you in a week."

-

Tim stood silently on the side of the chapel, trying his best to ignore the pain in his leg. Despite the warnings from the doctor to keep the hard knee brace on at all time for a couple weeks following the surgery, he refused to wear it today. At the podium, Colonel Vorhees was speaking about the lives and service of the men of ODA 1312, but Tim didn't hear any of the words. It was as if someone had turned down the volume on the world, leaving him to his thoughts, all of which were just questions at this point. How had he managed to drag himself up to the river's edge? Where had Mike and Eli disappeared to? Why hadn't he been able to save them? Why had he lived and they hadn't?

He did his best to drive those questions down, at least for the moment, as he looked across the faces of the families left behind. His families. He had been in every one of their homes for cookouts or birthdays. He had helped Mike's oldest son get ready for varsity-football tryouts, and Rizzo rebuild the engine on a car for his niece. And now that was all gone. Washed away in the blink of an eye.

Colonel Vorhees finished his speech and stepped down from the podium. Tim swallowed hard and stepped forward. Slowly, he moved down the line of wives and mothers, looking each in the eye and handing her a folded flag. With each exchange, he desperately wished he could change places and bring their husbands and sons back. After delivering eleven flags, Tim returned to his place at the side of the room and studied the stained glass on the opposite wall. Each window depicted a scene of what it meant to be a soldier—duty, honor, sacrifice. In that moment, Tim felt the true weight of each of those words.

The service ended, and people began moving toward the rear of the chapel for their opportunity to pass their condolences to the families. Tim stayed in place, waiting for the crowd to die down. Matt walked up next to him.

"Hey, Tim. It's good to see you."

"Matt, thanks for coming. I know Frank and the team would appreciate it."

"I wouldn't have missed it for the world. How are you doing?" Matt asked.

"I'm OK. The surgery went well, so I should be back up and running in a month or so."

"Yeah, but how are you doing?"

"I'm fine."

"Tim."

Tim looked at Matt and broke down. Matt and Drew were

the only other people who had been there. The only people who understood. Wiping the tears from his eyes, Tim tugged at the bottom of his dress-uniform jacket to straighten it out and recompose himself.

"I'll be OK. It's just still a lot to process."

"It's a lot for me, and I only had the opportunity to know you guys for a little bit. I can't even begin to imagine what you're going through. Just make sure you're not going through it alone. I'll call and check in on you in a few days," Matt said, turning to leave.

"Thanks, Matt," Tim replied.

Eventually, the crowd died out and Tim slipped out the chapel's side door. As he walked across the parking lot to his truck, a voice called out behind him.

"Tim Wells, don't you think you can just sneak out of here."

Tim turned around and saw Mike's wife, Trish, walking toward him.

"The service was hard enough; I couldn't think of anything to say to you all that didn't sound cliché."

"Tim, I don't need you to say anything," Trish said as she closed the distance between them. "I just need you to not blame yourself for everything, and don't act like you're not. It's written all over your face as clear as day. Mike is gone, and I will never stop missing him. But we are still here. Mike would have wanted us to live our lives as best we can. That's what I need you to do."

"I don't even know where to start," Tim admitted. "I'm totally lost here."

"You start right here—right where you are. Don't pretend you're not at rock bottom. Accept that this is where you are, and start working your way back. It won't be quick, and it won't be easy. But if you want to honor the memory of Mike and the rest of the team, that's what you'll do." Trish put her arms around him and squeezed. "The bad news, though, is that you're stuck with me now. If you thought Mike was tough, just you wait. If I find out you're not out there living your life and making the most of every moment there's going to be hell to pay."

Tim looked down at the diminutive woman and laughed. "Yes ma'am."

"Good answer. Now, I'm going home. Text me tomorrow so I know you're OK."

"Yes ma'am."

Tim watched as Trish walked back to her car, where her three kids were waiting. After she had driven off, he got into his truck and started the engine. He knew she was right. None of the team would accept him wallowing in self-pity. Right then and there, Tim resolved to live a life big enough for twelve.

-

Drew turned off the ignition and got out of her car. She breathed deeply, taking in the saltwater breeze. Pulling her backpack from the passenger seat, she got her bearings and walked down toward the docks filled with rows upon rows of boats. She turned down the pier marked "G" and continued along the wooden dock, admiring the different styles of boats as she went. Although she hadn't grown up around them, she had always been enamored by boats, and some of her favorite childhood memories were from times she'd been lucky enough to get a ride on one.

"I see you found it," a familiar voice called out.

Drew looked down the row and saw Matt standing on the bow of a sailboat three slips down from her.

"I've had opportunities to practice my navigation skills recently. It now seems to have come in handy," she replied.

"I'll say. Here, hand me your bag and climb aboard," Matt said, extending his hand to grasp the shoulder strap of the backpack.

"Thank you. This is such a beautiful boat!"

"She's a little older, but I wouldn't trade her for anything in the world. If you want to put this inside, I'll untie us and we can get out of here. Sound good?"

"You're the captain. Or . . . major? How does that work on here?"

"How about we just stick with *Matt*."

"OK. You're the Matt." Drew smiled and made her way down the side of the deck, through the cockpit, and down into the salon below.

She set her backpack on a seat in front of a small desk and looked around at the books and charts that lined the shelves. Overhead, she heard Matt moving around. A moment later, she saw his legs hop down into the cockpit and slip behind the wheel. Slowly, he reversed out of the slip and motored out of the harbor channel.

Drew climbed the three steps up into the cockpit. Leaning back against the cabin bulkhead facing the stern of the boat, she watched as Matt maneuvered the forty-foot sailboat around other boats and into the open water of the Chesapeake.

"Here's our mark," Matt said.

She watched as he pulled on several lines to hoist the sails, tightening them off using the boat's two drum winches. After a couple more minor adjustments, he stepped back behind the wheel.

"And now for my favorite part," he said, turning off the engine. Drew hadn't noticed the amount of noise the small diesel engine made while it was running, but now that it was off, she couldn't believe the difference.

Matt adjusted his course to take the boat across the bay toward Oxford, engaged the autopilot, and sat back against the stern railing. Drew watched him for a moment, and then walked back to sit next to him. He unwrapped his arm from the railing, and put it around her shoulder, pulling her tightly into his side.

Drew closed her eyes and sighed heavily, releasing weeks of tension in a single breath. She kept her eyes closed and listened to the sound of the water rushing along the hull and the wind singing in the rigging. And she listened to the sound of Matt's breathing. She had always known that men like him were out there in some abstract sense: men who exist in the shadows, willing to do whatever it took to keep people like her safe. But now she had found one of these men. Or maybe he had found her. Either way, he'd saved her life at least twice. Pressed against his chest, she felt a sense of safety that she was sure she would never find anywhere else. Matt shifted, and Drew opened her eyes to find him looking down at her, smiling. She knew this was where she belonged, and she was never going to give it up.

About the Author

Tom Gaines is an army officer who has spent his career at the intersection of technology and special operations. Now, he spends his time helping others learn to solve their own problems and telling stories.